W9-BFC-396

The Kiln

MacCartney

Read the other exciting books in the
Fire-us Trilogy!

BOOK 1: THE KINDLING

BOOK 2: THE KEEPERS OF THE FLAME

TRILOGY: BOOK 3

JENNIFER ARMSTRONG AND NANCY BUTCHER

An Imprint of HarperCollins*Publishers*

The Kiln

For information address HarperCollins Children's Books, a division of HarperCollins Publishers, 1350 Avenue of the Americas, New York, NY 10019.
www.harperteen.com

Library of Congress Cataloging-in-Publication Data
Armstrong, Jennifer.
The kiln / by Jennifer Armstrong and Nancy Butcher.
p. cm. — (Fire-us trilogy ; Book 3)
Summary: After a virus destroys most of the world's adult population, a band of children travels in search of an explanation for the dark mystery that forms the heart of their existence.
ISBN 0-06-008050-7 — ISBN 0-06-029413-2 (lib. bdg.)
[1. Survival—Fiction. 2. Science fiction.] I. Butcher, Nancy. II. Title.
PZ7.A73367 Kg 2002 2002006382
[Fic]—dc21 CIP
AC

1 2 3 4 5 6 7 8 9 10

First Edition

To my First Mommy and First Daddy,
I couldn't have made it without you
—J.A.

For Christopher
—N.B.

The Kiln

Do not begin this ~~test~~ Testing until instructed to do so. Use a number two pencil.

—The Book, page 176

Chapter One

"In late breaking news, the gang of orphans who recently did battle with the Keepers of the Flame—and by the way that was a sweet, *sweet* win, kids, hats off to you from all of us here in the newsroom!—have just been informed by a friendly old lady named Kirsten that a safe haven awaits them at this lovely golf-centered retirement community; and if you look up ahead you can see old ladies, lots of old ladies, sitting on the verandah, yet another group of Grown-ups—just for something new and different, something you don't see every day—just look at those lush putting greens and quite a herd of goats, too, and only two alligators sunning themselves today and why wouldn't the alligators be happy—I bet they get plenty of kid to eat—oops, sorry, Teddy, did I get your goat with that one? My, this sure is a nice—"

Nice, nice, nice, nice, nice, it's sooooo nice! Isn't it nice? Oh, yes, it's so nice!

"Shut up!" Angerman broke off his breakneck monologue to jab his elbow against his backpack. The point of his knobby elbow whacked with a sharp crack against the scarred and dented mannequin head inside, and Angerman winced with pain: Bad Guy always managed to get back at him, one way or another. Beside him on the golf cart, Mommy broke off her conversation with the white-haired old lady called Kirsten and gave him a warning frown.

Angerman let out a fainthearted laugh and then plastered a wide, camera-pleasing smile on his face as he resumed speaking through an empty picture frame. "*Excuse me*, folks. It's been a long, long journey for these kids from Lazarus, but they've seen plenty of bee-yootiful Florida scenery on the way! Too bad about that whole Keepers thing back in Jacksonville, but Cory is a welcome addition to this band of intrepid pilgrims, especially since it turns out she's Puppy and Kitty's auntie! The journey continues, and at the rate they're going, it shouldn't take them more than another two years to get all the way to Washington, D.C., our nation's—"

The Secret Service won't let you within a hundred yards of the president, punk—what makes you think different? They'll take one look at you and say, yup, here comes trouble!

"Shut up!"

No, you *shut up, kid! I've had just about* enough *of your lip! If you don't pipe down I'm going to get you good.*

Angerman wriggled the backpack straps off his shoulders and dug inside with one arm, dragging the head out. Bad Guy stared back at him with blank, painted eyes, but Angerman wasn't fooled by the innocent expression. Bad Guy had been getting more and more aggressive over the past few days, and Angerman couldn't even look at him without a tremor of fear making his shoulder blades twitch. The golf cart was slowing down, its solar batteries drained by their burden of one Grown-up, three teenagers, and six skinny children under ten.

The whine of the motor faded and stopped, and the

cart lurched to a halt on a circular gravel drive. Bad Guy tumbled out of Angerman's hand and landed on the ground with a thud.

Angerman giggled but then swallowed his laugh as Bad Guy hissed, *Do that again and I'll make you wish you'd never been born. You know what I'm capable of, right? So you watch yourself.* I *am.*

A cold shiver whipped up Angerman's back. Pressing his lips together, he jumped out of the cart and retrieved Bad Guy, stuffing the head into the backpack and snapping the buckles closed.

Kirsten stepped out of the golf cart as Mommy, Hunter, Teddy Bear, Action Figure, Baby, Doll, Puppy, and Kitty gawked at the sprawling campus of white stucco buildings, the thick tangle of creepers and vines that had pulled the gutters askew, the waist-high grasses and palmettos, the cement reflecting pool with its dead fountain and stagnant green water, the messy pelican nests, and the streaks of bird guano that striped the walls. "Welcome to the Woods," Kirsten said. "I'll tell Hannah you're here."

And then dozens of old women were tottering toward them—white-haired ladies pushing walkers; baby-stepping grandmas with arthritic, bony hands, others trying to sit up taller in their wheelchairs on the weed-studded patio to see what the commotion was, all of them staring from wrinkled faces with wide, astonished eyes. "Children!" came tremulous cries from every side. "Look! Real children!"

Teacher stood in the middle of the crossroads, chewing her lip with worry. Behind her, the sound of the surf was punctuated by gulls' cries, and the saw-toothed dune grasses bowed and whispered together. Teacher was aware of a bead of sweat rolling down her spine in short little swoops—bump, bump, bump over each jutting vertebra, and her hands on The Book were slick with moisture. Beside her, Cory stood straight as a flagpole, her jaw clenching and unclenching, clenching and unclenching. The Confederate cavalry officer's hat she'd been wearing since their stay at the Civil War museum cast a shadow down to her chin.

"They can't have gone far," Teacher said.

Cory didn't answer.

"Because Doll's dolly is still here and they didn't take any of the bikes," Teacher went on, turning to look at the beach house where they had spent the night. An assortment of bicycles was scattered in the shell-strewn front yard, some leaning against the porch railing, some toppled over, their kickstands useless in the soft sand. They were the bicycles they had stolen from the Crossroads, the mall that was home to the Keepers of the Flame, the only Grown-ups the kids had seen in five years—the first Grown-ups they'd seen since Fire-us had killed all the First Mommies and First Daddies and left the children to fend for themselves or die. It had been a cruel disappointment to discover that it wasn't safe to stay with the Keepers. And now that everyone had disappeared, just vanished, Teacher couldn't help worrying that the Keepers had come after them again and—

"Say the writing again," Cory said, breaking into Teacher's thoughts. Strands of blond hair had come loose from her thick braid and wafted back and forth across her face as the breeze kicked up. She tucked them up under her hat.

Teacher hefted the heavy scrapbook in her hands. It held clues and memories and pictures and all kinds of Information that Teacher had collected all these long years, pasting things in, writing down memories that they remembered in dreams, looking through it for answers to all their fears and predicaments. And now it held a message she'd never seen before, in a stranger's handwriting. She didn't need to look at it again to repeat the words.

"Over the river and through the woods, to grandmother's house we go," Teacher said, and through her head went a darting bird of a memory, a tune so far away that she couldn't quite catch it—and then it was gone.

"So they went to grandmother's house," Cory said. "Puppy and Kitty are at *grandmother*'s house."

"And everyone else, too," Teacher hastened to say. Cory shrugged one shoulder, her face impatient and fierce, and Teacher continued, "We have to figure out where that is. A grandmother, or somebody called Grandmother, came and took them away and left us this note."

"That letter that looks like this—" Cory held up three fingers and spread them apart. "That's the *w* sound, right? W-woods?"

Teacher frowned, feeling another bead of sweat start its bump-bump-bump down her bony back. "Cory, I know you're not so good at reading, but we don't really have time right now to do School."

"Woods," Cory repeated. She was squinting into the distance, up the road in the opposite direction they had ridden their bikes searching for food and water. She pointed. "Woods."

"There aren't any woods," Teacher said. "This is the beach, not—hey!"

She gasped as Cory grabbed her arm and swung her around to face the road.

"Woods!" Cory growled, pointing.

Hot and angry, Teacher looked up the road. Almost too far away to see was a faded sign. She shaded her eyes. "'The Woods: A Golf-Centered Retirement Community,'" she read. She gave Cory a sheepish look. "Sorry."

"That's where they are." Cory swung her leg over her bicycle and popped the kickstand. "Let's go."

Cory had a good head start as Teacher tucked The Book and Doll's dolly into the basket on her handlebars and jumped on her bicycle. Sand had drifted across the road, leaving nothing but a narrow path barely wide enough for two bicycles side by side. A lizard flicked across the hot pavement and into the dunes as the girls pedaled toward the sign up the road, and Teacher heard a far-off whine, a strange, mechanical or even electrical sound. It was a puzzling sound and hard to place, because she hadn't heard anything electrical in so long, wasn't even really sure it *was* an electrical sound. Just as they were about to turn up a winding drive that led over the dunes, a car came whirring out of it. Teacher and Cory both swerved impulsively, and Teacher caught a glimpse of Hunter's startled face as she skidded in the sand at the side of the road and went sprawling head over heels.

"Teacher!" he called out.

"I'm okay!" Wincing, Teacher picked herself up out of the deep, drifted sand. She had a scratch on one bare arm from the sharp grass and a greasy scrape on one shin from the bicycle chain, but on the whole she was unharmed. Her heart thumped with adrenaline.

Hunter climbed out of the vehicle he was driving and helped her up, sunlight flashing off his glasses.

"What is that?" she asked, clapping sand off her hands and shorts. "It's not a car, really."

"Golf cart," Hunter replied. "Works on solar power."

"Solar? From the sunshine?" Teacher gave the cart a quick once-over. "Mean it doesn't need any—"

"Puppy and Kitty okay?" Cory broke in.

Hunter nodded. "We're all up at the whatchama-callit, requirement home. I was coming back to see if you guys had showed up yet. We didn't want you to think we left you behind. Come on, get in," he said, gesturing toward the golf cart.

"Wait," Teacher said. She bent to retrieve The Book and doll from the sand. "Are there people up there? *Other* people? Grown-ups?"

Grinning, Hunter said, "It's all old ladies, Teacher, nothing but old ladies like a whole bunch of grandmas. Do you remember having a grandma?"

Teacher and Cory exchanged a worried glance. "Are you sure they're not Keepers?" Cory asked.

"They're just normal grandmas," Hunter said. "Really."

A whisper of uneasiness made Teacher avoid Hunter's eager gaze. Of all of them, he had been the one who was most enthusiastic about the Keepers in the beginning. There was something in Hunter that was desperate for Grown-up approval, yearning to have one pat him on the shoulder and tell him he was doing a good job. He had been the hunter forever, the man of the family long before Angerman ever showed up. But he was still a kid, they were all still just kids, and he wanted so much to find Grown-ups. She hoped he wasn't wrong again this time.

"There's one named Kirsten and one named Hannah—I think she's sort of in charge of the whole place," Hunter went on. "They don't have those weird Keeper names or anything. I don't know how come they're not dead like all the other Grown-ups—I mean, besides the Keepers. Some of them are really old, too, and all hunched over and some that I think maybe are a little bit sea-mile."

"Senile," Teacher corrected, chewing the edge of her thumbnail.

"Whatever. And they're just going nuts over the little ones, too, fighting over who gets to have one in her lap. I don't think Puppy and Kitty have set their feet on the ground since we got there."

"Let's go." Cory let her bicycle fall to the ground with a crash and climbed into the golf cart.

"How do you know how to drive this?" Teacher asked as Hunter put the cart into reverse and did a three-point turn across the road. The electric motor whined and hummed.

"Guys always know how to drive," Hunter said with a cheery grin. "The place is just over this big ridge of dunes."

As the golf cart crested the rise, Teacher turned and looked back, seeing the ocean spread out flat and sparkling all the way to the horizon and the dry, sandy rim of beach and road and storm-battered houses. Then she faced forward, and they dipped down toward a jungly tangle of green. What was once a manicured golf course of greens and lawns was now overgrown with scrub and tall, nodding grasses, and the former water hazards were now lagoons half clogged with marsh plants and algae. Pink flamingoes stood around on one leg with their heads under their wings.

Rounding a bend, they came upon a velvety sward of short, clipped meadow, and Teacher felt the shock of recognition: *lawnmowers, and shrieking on a barefoot dash through the sprinkler's rainbow spray, and the sound of a car door slamming in the driveway . . .*

But then she saw dozens of dainty goats whisking their tails and nibbling the grass, and she knew that *of course* there was no lawnmower and no sprinkler and no Daddy coming home from work and swooping her up into the blue, blue air in a big bear hug. . . .

Teacher hated it—the way those memories snuck up on her when she least expected it, when she couldn't brace herself against the heartache. She gripped The Book in her lap and squeezed her arms close to her ribs.

Then the buildings came into view—a cluster of low, white stucco houses with red tile roofs—and a circular driveway with three palm trees leaning out at odd angles in the grassy center. A goat with knobby little horns was tied by a long tether to one of the trees, and it was busy cropping the grass neat and short. Five golf carts just like the one Hunter was driving were parked at the entrance. With the clipped grass, and the golf carts, and the raked gravel driveway, the place looked almost like a

Before Time place—*almost*, because in spite of the attempt to keep it tidy and neat, it was being invaded by plants. Bougainvillea in scarlet and bright pink cascaded in great, viny plumes over the roofs and walls, palmettos pushed up through a cement patio, and pepper bushes pressed close to the windows, splay fingered and spiky. Goats had nibbled everything within reach, leaving the shrubs bare legged and naked at the bottom, but the lush vegetation kept growing up and above wherever the goats couldn't stretch.

The golf cart crunched over gravel, its motor whining. Hunter pulled the cart in at the end of the row and switched it off. Quiet fell like a shadow over the three teenagers in the cart, and then the goat under the palm trees raised its stub-horned head and bleated, *"Maaaaaa!"*

"This is it," Hunter said. "The grandmas are all inside."

Chapter Two

Mommy stood in the doorway of the Sunshine Room and blinked into the light pouring through the picture window. There were grandmas everywhere, moving around in wheelchairs, teetering on canes, fussing over her family, beaming toothless smiles at all the children. Doll was singing her silly songs to a grandma named Helen, who kept squeezing Doll's arm and muttering "Henry, Henry." Baby was running around in something called a muu-muu, which one of the grandmas had given her. It had big yellow flowers on it and dragged along behind her. Action Figure was sitting on the lap of a hunched-over grandma named Con-Sue-Ella, who was showing the boy how to turn the wheelchair one way and then the other. Mommy resisted the impulse to warn Con-Sue-Ella that this was not a good idea, since Action Figure was so wild. Con-Sue-Ella looked so happy that Mommy couldn't bring herself to do it.

Puppy and Kitty were sitting on an overstuffed couch on either side of Angerman, under a poster that said *YOU'RE NOT GETTING OLDER, YOU'RE GETTING BETTER!* They were staring at the doorway and fidgeting—wondering where Cory was, no doubt. Hunter had gone off in one of those electric carts to fetch Cory and Teacher at the beach house. Mommy wondered what was taking him so long.

Teddy Bear was picking things up from the glass

coffee table—a small brown plastic bottle with a label on it, a magazine called *Scientific American*—and putting them down again. He, like the twins, had his eye on the doorway. He hated being separated from Teacher, who was his big sister from the Before Time. Two grandmas dressed in stained hospital gowns stood behind him and stroked his hair, and exchanged words that made no sense to Mommy: *muchacho lindo, demasiado fino!* He paid no attention to the sour, unwashed smell of them.

All these grandmas! Mommy frowned and tried to remember her own grandma or grandmas. That would have been her First Mommy's mother and her First Daddy's mother. But it was so hard. Mommy couldn't even remember her own name, or anything about her First Mommy or First Daddy either. None of them could, really—at least those memories were so fuzzy it was hard to know if they were real or just dreams. Although when she and Hunter and the others had left Lazarus, which had been their home since Fire-us, they had found a book with the name Annie Ginkel written in it in a car that Mommy thought might be her First Family's car.

Annie Ginkel. Grandma Ginkel. In her mind, Mommy saw—or felt, rather—a papery-soft hand holding hers. In church. And smelled the warm, dusty smell of make-up powder. And heard a voice saying, *Honey, we'll go to the Friendly's after this borin' sermon's over and treat ourselves to a coupla hot fudge sundaes. We girls deserve that, don't we?*

"Can I get you something to eat?"

Mommy blinked into the light and saw the grandma named Nana standing in front of her. Her real name was Hannah, but she had insisted on being called Nana.

Nana seemed to be younger than the other grandmas. She was tall and slender with short gray-black hair and big brown eyes and a smile full of shiny white teeth. She was dressed in khaki pants and a shirt with a cartoon mouse on it.

Mommy pointed at the mouse. "Who is that? Teddy has a shirt with him on it, too."

"That's Mickey Mouse, from Disney World," Nana said. "Do you remember Disney World, dear?"

Mommy scrunched up her face. "Not really."

"I used to take my brother's grandkids. It was a fun place. Probably overrun by wild animals now, and not cartoon ones, either." Nana held out her hand. "So. Why don't we get you a little something to eat?"

"'kay."

Mommy let Nana lead her over to the couch across from where Angerman and the twins were sitting. On the table between the two couches was a platter with bread and some white, soft-looking thing that smelled pungent and another platter piled high with big red berries. Nearby, a grandma was sitting in a chair by herself and staring at the blank screen of a TV set, her lips moving soundlessly and a thread of drool running down her chin. Nana wiped it away with a tender gesture.

"Is she . . . okay?" Mommy asked Nana. "What's her name?"

"Gladys." Nana patted Gladys's cheek. "She's my mother."

Mommy stared. "Your real mommy?"

"Yes, my real mommy," Nana replied with a sad smile. "Although she doesn't remember that she is my mommy. She has Alzheimer's—a lot of the women here do. It's a disease that makes you confused. It makes you forget everything about your past."

"We don't remember our pasts. Does that mean we have that All Zymer's, too?" Mommy asked.

"No, dear, you don't. I'm a doctor, so I'd know."

"You're a doctor?" Mommy exclaimed. "A real doctor?"

Nana nodded. "I was the resident doctor here at the Woods. Had been, for twenty years, ever since I moved my mother here. It's lucky, too, because I was able to take care of these women after they lost their husbands and the other staff members died and—" She broke off and forced a smile. "Why don't you help yourself to some food?"

"Yes." Mommy reached over to the platter of big red berries. She couldn't get over the fact that Nana had her own real mommy still with her. "Is this a strawberry?" she said in wonder.

Nana laughed. "Yes, ma'am."

"I haven't had one of these since . . . wow, where'd you get it?"

"We have a garden out back," Nana explained. "We also have a hydroponic greenhouse, where we grow vegetables and fruits in special chemicals. I can show you later. And the cheese is made from goat's milk, from our goats."

"Cheese," Mommy repeated. It stirred a memory—mackincheese, something she used to eat in the Before Time.

Nana frowned. "What have you children been eating all these years?"

"Hunter's been hunting for us, at the Publix and

Winn-Dixie and stuff," Mommy replied. "Peanut butter and canned tuna and whatever else the animals didn't get first. Powdered milk."

"I see."

Mommy felt Nana scrutinizing her hair, her face, her eyes. "We need to increase your vitamin C intake. All of you."

"I know what that is, vitamin see. I had Hunter to hunt vitamins for us, so we wouldn't get sick."

"You're a very smart young lady. Go ahead, now, eat."

Mommy picked up a strawberry and bit into it. It tasted like . . . she searched her memory. Like birthday cake. Like a picnic in the park on a beautiful spring day. The tiny seeds crunched inside her mouth.

"You like that, huh?" Nana grinned.

"Yes," Mommy said. And then she remembered to do Manners. "Thank you."

Nana watched Mommy for a second, then turned to Puppy and Kitty. "Twins, right? How old are they?" she asked.

Mommy didn't answer. She remembered how interested the Keepers had been in Puppy and Kitty. So interested, in fact, that they had kidnapped the twins and locked them up in a cage, and would have taken them away for Testing, if Mommy had not rescued them in time. Mommy still wasn't sure what Testing was, exactly, or where the Testing place was. But in any case, she was the mommy of the family, and she had to keep all her little ones safe.

Nana seemed to notice Mommy's silence. "I'm sorry, you're probably feeling a little overwhelmed," she said.

"We can talk later. We have a lot of questions for you kids, and I'm sure you have a lot of questions for us. It's just been so long since we've seen . . ." She smiled. "Children. Such sweet, pretty children. It's been just us old gals, all these years since the viral outbreak."

"Viral outbreak!"

Mommy glanced up sharply at the sound of Angerman's voice.

"This just in," Angerman said, jumping to his feet and grabbing the frame.

Puppy and Kitty cringed. Gladys, the grandma who had been watching the broken TV set, turned around and regarded Angerman with watery blue eyes, almost as if with relief that the TV had finally come on again.

"Angerman," Mommy warned.

"Did someone say viral outbreak?" Angerman went on. "Hey, my favorite subject! Okay, all right, what has two legs and two arms and a temperature of 107 degrees Fahrenheit and is screaming for help except that there's no more strawberry I scream and no more medicine, either, and all the doctors in Washington, D.C., are—*ow*!"

Angerman stopped talking. His hands shot up to his chin. "Let . . . go," he whispered, working his fingers around his neck. "Can't . . . breathe."

Nana set down another bowl of fruit with a thump on the table and strode to Angerman's side, but Mommy put her hand out to stop her. "He's just—you know—acting that way."

"Now, Angerman, cut it out!" Mommy scolded. He had always been crazy. But he had been getting even crazier these last few days, since their escape from the Crossroads.

"Are you okay?" Nana said, ignoring Mommy and staring at Angerman.

Angerman gulped down a deep breath. Then he folded his arms in front of his chest so tightly that his knuckles showed white. "Uh-huh. I am all right, thank you for asking, Nana. Everyone go about your business, there's nothing to—*hmfggg.*" He gasped and stopped talking again.

Puppy began to bark. He didn't speak real words most of the time, and neither did Kitty. Mommy got up from her seat and snuggled in between the twins. Angerman fell to his knees and began gulping down strawberries, two at a time.

The twins scrunched up close. Mommy kissed their heads, which were sweaty and salty tasting. They needed baths. "It's okay," she murmured. "Here, how about some strawberries? Angerman, save some for the little kids, okay?"

All of a sudden, Puppy and Kitty squirmed away from her and jumped off the couch. "Hey, where're you going?" Mommy called out.

And then Mommy saw that Hunter, Teacher, and Cory had arrived. They were standing in the doorway of the Sunshine Room. Teacher was hugging The Book to her chest and glancing around with a stunned expression. Doll's dolly poked out from underneath her arm. Cory hovered behind Teacher, until she saw the twins come running up. "Hey, guys!" she cried out as they flung their arms around her legs.

Nana rose to her feet and walked up to Teacher and Cory. Helen and Kirsten and Con-Sue-Ella and some of the other grandmas followed in a traffic jam of walkers and wheelchairs. "Welcome, girls!" Nana called out. "Welcome to the Woods!"

Teacher caught Mommy's eye and mouthed the words *What's going on?* Mommy wasn't sure how to answer.

"So we've been traveling north for a long time," Hunter explained to the grandmas. "Weeks, probably. Or maybe months."

"Where're you all from originally?" Nana asked him.

Hunter squirmed. He glanced at Mommy, who was squeezed between him and Nana on the couch, and then at Teacher and Cory, who sat cross-legged on the red tile floor. Teacher and Cory weren't talking much, mostly just staring around the Sunshine Room at all the grandmas.

"Well, we're not sure about that," Hunter said, taking off his glasses and rubbing his eyes. "See, after Fire-us, me and Action . . . that's my little brother over there."

"Action?" Kirsten broke in. "His name is Action?"

"Well, Action Figure," Hunter explained. "I guess that's not a real name, but somehow I couldn't remember. I mean, I got confused—"

Nana patted his hand. "Action is a fine name. Go on."

"Well, after Fire-us, we wandered around for a while, and then settled down at this car repair place, where there was a lot of canned food and clothes that fit and other stuff. That was in Lazarus, down south. And then Teacher and Teddy found us. And then the four of us found Mommy and the girls living in a house on Mango Street that used to belong to some First Family who, uh . . ."

"Died," Mommy said in a low voice.

"Yeah, that. Died. We've been a family all these years. I'm the hunter, and Mommy's the mommy, and Teacher the teacher. She does School almost every day. For the little kids."

Kirsten walked up to them and perched on one of the armrests. "What about that odd fella there, the one with the long brown hair?" she whispered. She nodded at Angerman, who was rocking back and forth in a white wicker rocking chair and muttering over his shoulder at Bad Guy.

"That's Angerman," Teacher spoke up. "He joined our family not that long ago. He just kinda showed up on our doorstep like that. We don't know too much about him or where he's from."

"And the twins came just after that," Mommy added.

"Angerman talked us all into going to Washington, D.C.," Hunter went on. "So I hunted for supplies, and we hit the road. First we rode bikes. Then we canoed up a river, to Jacksonville. And then the Keepers found us."

"Who are these Keepers?" Nana asked.

"They're crazy people," Cory blurted out. "I used to live with them at this mall called the Crossroads, and they changed my name to Corinthians 1:19, and they wanted to do bad things to . . ." She glanced over at Puppy and Kitty. "Anyway, we got away from them. Deuteronomy 29:28 and Daniel 7:15 chased us in their chariots all the way up the highway, but we got away from them."

She paused and touched her head, where a scab-crusted bruise was partly covered by her blond hair. Hunter remembered that she'd hurt herself saving

Puppy and Kitty and Action Figure from the Keepers. He realized with a start that he owed Cory for his brother's life. She was so brave.

"Well, how perfectly awful," Nana murmured. "We've never seen these Keeper people around here. And I hope we never will." She added, "But back up a second. You said you're headed up to Washington, D.C.? Whatever for? That's a long way from here."

Doll, who was sprawled out on the floor playing pretend games with Baby, held her dolly up to her face. "We're looking for the prisoner of the United States," Doll squeaked.

"That's President," Teacher corrected her. "President of the United States. Don't you remember, from School?"

"Prisoner," Doll insisted.

Teacher sighed and shrugged. "Angerman thought that if we could find President, we'd get some answers about what happened," she explained to Nana and Kirsten. "Like how Fire-us started and why all the Grown-ups died."

Mommy blinked at the two grandmas. "Except for you guys. And the Keepers, too. You're all Grown-ups, and you didn't die."

"Yes, well . . ." Nana began.

"Do you know where the prisoner of the United States is?" Baby asked Nana.

"Well, if he's still alive he's probably in Washington, D.C.," Nana replied. "But he could also be at Pisgah Island. But I don't believe he's alive at all."

"What? What did you say about Pisgah?" Cory demanded. The welt on her forehead seemed to darken as her face went white.

"Pisgah Island," Nana repeated. "It's the presidential retreat, about thirty miles up the coast. The president and his family used to take vacations there, before—"

"Pisgah! That's where Sup-eam Reader lives," Doll piped up. She held up her dolly. "Sup-eam Reader's gonna give you a test!"

"No, nuh-uh, Sup-eam Reader's gonna give Puppy and Kitty a test!" Baby corrected her. "I wonder is he gonna give 'em grades, like Teacher does?"

Cory rose to her feet abruptly and walked over to the window, where she stared out at the overgrown green lawn. Mommy ran after her, saying, "Cory, Cory, it's gonna be okay. . . ."

Nana frowned at Hunter. "I don't understand. What is all this business about a Sup-eam Reader?"

"Supreme Leader," Hunter said. He glanced across the room at Puppy and Kitty, who were sitting on some grandma's lap and drinking grape juice out of beer mugs. "He's the leader of the Keepers."

"According to Cory, he and a bunch of other Keepers live in some place called Pisgah," Teacher said. She put The Book on her lap and began trailing her fingers across the cover, back and forth, back and forth, as if searching for answers. "Which means that maybe this Pisgah Island place, which used to belong to President, belongs to the Keepers now."

Angerman stopped rocking and raised his hand and opened his mouth to speak.

"What?" Teacher said. "What is it, Angerman?"

Angerman moved his lips, but no sound came out.

Chapter Three

Cory's eyebrows rose into an arch as she watched Angerman opening and closing his mouth like a fish out of water. The old ladies kept smiling, as if they expected that any moment now, Angerman would turn out to be a normal boy. The silence stretched, and then was broken by a plaintive, trembling voice.

"I can't hear what he's saying, Gloria, what is he saying?"

"Nothing, he's not saying anything," another grandma snapped. "That's the trouble with young people these days, always grabbing attention and then not having a darn thing to—"

"How do you *know* the president isn't alive?" Hunter blurted out, looking at Nana. "He could even be at Pisgah."

"Yeah," Mommy chimed in. "Did you go look for him?"

Nana picked up the handkerchief that a lady on the cracked vinyl sofa had dropped and pressed it back into her hand. "You dropped your hankie again, Elizabeth. No," she said, turning back to the kids. "Those of us who are—or were—strong enough to go couldn't leave the others. Everything was sheer chaos for such a long time. And then, well, I guess we never really thought about it. There didn't seem to be any point in going off on a wild-goose chase."

A thin squeak came from Angerman. Then he clapped his hands over his mouth. Nana tipped her head. "Are you—?"

"He'll be okay," Teacher explained. She went over to sit beside him on the arm of his chair, and put a hand on his shoulder. Angerman turned his face to her with a beseeching look. "He'll be okay," she said, although her voice was less than confident.

"He's getting a complete physical exam as soon as possible," Nana said in a no-nonsense tone. "That goes for all of you."

"But what about Pisgah?" Hunter pressed. "You never wanted to see if the president was there?"

"Hunter," Nana began. Then she interrupted herself, gesturing outside with her head. "Let's take a walk. All of you older kids. The little ones can stay inside and play."

While Teacher took Angerman by the arm and led him outside, Cory shrugged and pushed herself up from the floor where she'd been sitting with Puppy and Kitty. "You stay here," she whispered to them. "I'll be right back."

Nana slid the glass door shut behind them as they filed out onto the cracked cement patio. Mommy stood, hugging her arms around herself. Hunter worked a piece of rubble loose from the patio with his toe and then shoved it back into place, looking a little sheepish. Angerman shuffled sideways to hide behind a trailing vine and peeked out between the leaves, shaking his head as Teacher tried to coax him out. Nana stared out across the meadow, where the goats ambled in twos and threes, and then drew a deep breath.

"Kids, do you know anything about what happened five years ago? The virus?"

"The Great Flame," Cory said under her breath.

"We thought it was called Fire-us," Teacher said, "because—because it seemed like—"

"Like people burned up?" Nana asked. She gave them all a tender look. "What you must have been through. Well, let me see if I can explain."

Cory noticed Teacher hug her big scrapbook to her chest in an almost convulsive gesture, but she didn't open it. They all—except Angerman—took seats on the low masonry wall that surrounded the patio. It was a peaceful scene, with the sun filtering through the blossoming vines and glowing on the stucco buildings, with the occasional bleat of a goat in the distance. Nana rubbed her hands on the knees of her faded pants, shaking her head.

"I'm a doctor, I told you that. I had just retired from my own practice and become the resident doctor here at the Woods because I specialized in geriatric medicine—that means taking care of old people's health. For a long time after the epidemic I had this suspicion about how the virus worked, and you kids showing up here makes me pretty sure I'm right."

"But what is it?" Mommy asked. "What is Fire—I mean virus?"

"It's a kind of germ," Nana said. "All viruses are much too small to see with your eyes, but they come in lots of different shapes, and they do different kinds of things when they get inside a human body. Some viruses attach themselves to—oh, say, red blood cells or brain tissue—or they work best in the chemical environment of the kidneys, for example, or they seek out something that the body produces inside and use it for their own needs. Every virus has a different habit, but the main thing a virus tries to do is survive and reproduce itself and make more virus."

They all looked up as Teddy Bear tapped on a window and waved, and then darted away with a big grin. Through the glass, Cory could see Kitty and Puppy digging their index fingers into the soft goat cheese and licking it off. She smiled and turned back. Nana was still speaking.

"The kind of virus that we had—the epidemic—it affected adults. But not old women. No children under the age of puberty, and no women past menopause." Nana stopped, seeing the blank looks. "Oh dear, you don't know anything about—about what happens in your body when you— Haven't any of you girls begun to menstruate?"

Cory and Teacher and Mommy all looked at one another, and then back to Nana.

"When you become a woman," Nana began.

"Oh!" Cory cried out, and then clamped her mouth shut, her face hot. "I didn't know it was called that," she mumbled.

Hunter was staring at her, as were the other girls. "What?" Teacher whispered, her eyes bugging. "What is it?"

"Never mind," Cory said through gritted teeth. At the Crossroads, she had been taught that the bleeding was the curse of Eve and that it was womankind's punishment for original sin. When it had first happened to her, she had felt the sting of shame and guilt. And then the Keepers had started to prepare her to become a Handmaid, and she was allowed to go seek her Visioning.

"Let me just explain about the virus first," Nana said. "We'll get to the birds and the bees later. For now, you just have to understand that when you reach a certain age, your body begins to make a kind of chemical called a sexual hormone, and it means you can make babies. Men continue to produce this in their bodies for the rest of their lives, but after a certain age, maybe fifty or fifty-five, women's bodies stop making it. My theory is that the virus only affected people with those hormones. All of the men who were here died, and the women who were taking artificial hormones for some symptoms they had, they died, too. And now I see that you kids survived—"

Nana looked away, a deep crease in her forehead. "But why aren't there any other children?" she wondered aloud.

The kids were silent for a moment, and a breeze shook a handful of red blossoms from the vine and scattered them on the patio. The flowers lay like bright drops of blood on the cement.

In a low voice, Mommy said, "A lot of other children died later. From hunger or getting hurt or getting sick. Different things. Wild animals," she added, her voice dropping to a whisper.

The doctor shook her head, regarding them all, her brown eyes sorrowful. "I don't know how you managed to stay alive all by yourselves. But the fact that the virus didn't make you sick confirms my theory."

A sickening realization turned Cory cold. "Is it—is it still out there? I mean, if you can get sick from it once you—once you do that men-street thing."

"I don't think so," Nana said. "That virus was

incredibly hot. That means it spread like wildfire, jumping from one person to another to another. But once it had killed every susceptible person it came into contact with it burned itself out, like a fire that has no more wood. And, besides, weren't those Keepers you talked about, weren't they adults? They would have gotten sick by now if it was still out there in the environment. I suppose they were somehow isolated during the whole outbreak, otherwise they'd be dead, too. Like all the others.

"So you see," Nana continued in a gentle voice. "I don't think the president could still be alive. The president was always surrounded by crowds of people. So he would have gotten sick right away. I don't see how there's any way the president could be at Pisgah or in Washington or anywhere else, for that matter. He must be dead."

Angerman wanted to step out from behind the flowering vine, but every time he tried to make a move, Bad Guy hissed at him to stay still. Nana's voice reached him like gentle waves on the beach, soft crescendos of words and then a fading away. Some of it he heard clearly, but with Bad Guy muttering at him, it was hard to follow Nana's explanation. Instead of listening, he concentrated on sneaking out of his hiding place without Bad Guy noticing. While he figured the head was busy listening to Nana, Angerman eased himself a half inch at a time, stopping whenever Nana's voice faded again. At last, he lunged the rest of the way out just as Nana said, "He must be dead."

"Listen!" Angerman blurted out.

They all turned their heads to stare at him. Angerman could feel the rage and power from Bad Guy like a bonfire behind him: the head didn't have to say a word for him to know he was in big trouble if he breathed a word.

Mommy rose from her seat and took a step toward him. "What, Angerman? We're listening."

"Nothing. Sorry," Angerman mumbled.

He saw Nana frowning at him, sizing him up. He kept his head down, stealing quick glances through his tumbled hair, and at last the woman shook her head and looked away from him.

"I think you should all stay with us here," Nana said. "I understand that you've been searching for answers, I understand that need, believe me. But I don't think you'll find any more answers than what I've just told you. There's nothing out there for you to find."

Watch yourself kid, Bad Guy whispered as Angerman raised his eyes to Nana's face.

"Well . . ." Teacher began. "I guess if the others want to . . ."

"You're safe here," Nana continued. "We have vegetables, cheese, milk. And I won't try to deny we could really use your help, all you strong young kids. I've got some engineering projects in mind, but I can't implement them on my own."

As Hunter and Mommy, Teacher and Cory discussed the idea with the doctor, Angerman slowly shrugged the backpack off his shoulders. The patio door slid open, and the little kids came out, streaming past Angerman, full of chatter. Baby and Doll wanted to play with the baby goats, and Action Figure announced he was going to ride one.

Slowly, slowly, as the happy voices and laughter swirled around him, Angerman lowered the backpack to the ground beside a lounge chair. If he was lucky, the confusion and noise would cover up his actions. If he could just get away from Bad Guy, maybe he'd be able to talk without fear that he was being spied on. Angerman took a step away, and then another, and he was beginning to think this would work, when Puppy climbed up onto the lounge chair and reached for the backpack. His heart pounding, Angerman bolted for the pack and snatched it away from the boy.

Awww, I wouldn't hurt the little tyke, Bad Guy said with a nasty chuckle. *Besides, you really thought you could get away with that? Give the old man some credit for having a brain, kiddo. I ain't got no body; but I do have a head on your shoulders. Besides, I didn't get where I am today without knowing a thing or two about human nature.*

Fear and frustration settled on Angerman like two crows perching on his shoulders. He hardly dared move in case they began pecking his eyes out. He couldn't let Bad Guy out of his sight, but as long as he was near, Angerman would never be able to speak the truth.

Dinner preparations were under way. Teacher could hear Mommy and Hunter chatting with some of the grandmas in the big kitchen down the hall. She could hear words like *salad* and *melted cheese*, and they filled Teacher with happiness and delicious memories of the Before Time. She whispered "*salad*" to herself as she examined her treasure trove.

Spread out in front of her on a table were books—

lots of books. Unburned. Not spoiled by damp and mold. Not chewed on by rats. Just plain, nice books. Teacher had her hands clasped in her lap, holding herself back. At first, she just allowed herself to look at the covers and read the titles—titles like *Meditations for the End of Day*, *Fit and Fabulous After Fifty!*, *Northanger Abbey*—and wonder what might be inside.

As she was enjoying the anticipation, there was a bump and thump in the doorway, and Action Figure crashed through in a wheelchair, his hands pushing away at the wheel grips. "Winnin'!" He panted.

"Careful, Action," Teacher said before turning back to her books.

With another crash and bump, he maneuvered his way out through the opposite door. Somebody out in the hallway cried out in surprise, as though a wheelchair had just run over her foot.

"Remind me to hide the keys to the golf carts," Kirsten said, bustling through with a basket of carrots.

Teddy Bear rolled into the room in another wheelchair, awkward with the motions and sticking his tongue out of the corner of his mouth with the effort. "'ction go this way?"

"Be careful, Teddy," Teacher warned him. She watched as he worked his way through the opposite door, chasing Action Figure.

At last, Teacher reached out and pulled one book toward her: *What You Need to Know About Osteoporosis*. It sounded important, and Teacher had always been careful to find out what she needed to know. Osteoporoses might be some kind of dangerous animals, or horrorcanes, or some other tricky thing they might need to be cautious of. She was prepared to write down everything, even rip out the pages if necessary and glue them into her scrapbook. After all, she never knew when a piece of Information in The Book would come in handy.

But there were so many books here—how would she get all of this into The Book? Then Teacher began to laugh.

"It's already in a book," she said out loud. "I don't have to write it down."

Grinning, she opened to page one of the osteoporosis manual and began to read.

Chapter Four

"Once upon a time, there was a princess who lived in a castle. Her name was Sleeping Birdy, and she liked to sleep a lot. She had two strep-sisters, Oprah and Rosie, who liked to watch TV."

Hunter sat back in his chair and let Mommy's quiet voice wash over him. He knew the bedtime story was supposed to be for the little ones, but it was making him sleepy, too. Hunter liked this room, which was connected to the big kids' bedroom by a doorway. The walls were painted light blue, like the sky, and his chair was soft and comfortable.

"Mommy, what's TV?" Baby murmured. She shifted around under the white cotton blanket until she was curled up in a ball. She was lying between Mommy and Doll on the big bed. Puppy and Kitty were on the other side of Mommy.

"It's like what Angerman does when he gives the news," Mommy explained, stroking Baby's blond curls. "Doll, scoot over so Puppy and Kitty have more room."

"Dolly needs room, too," Doll protested, clutching her doll to her chest.

"I know that, honey, but Puppy and Kitty are right at the edge of the bed. Move over just a little bit, okay? There, that's it. Action and Teddy, you guys comfy over there?"

"Yes, Mommy," Teddy Bear's voice drifted over from

the twin bed the two boys shared.

"Resta story!" Action Figure demanded.

"Okay, all right. So one day, this prince named, um, George in a Bush said, 'I believe in the family.' So he came around to Sleeping Birdy's castle looking for a princess to marry."

"Wedding dress," Doll mumbled, her eyelids drooping.

"That's right, honey, a princess in a wedding dress. So everyone went to the two-for-one sale at Our Lord and Taylor . . ."

A warm breeze blew in through the open window, carrying with it the heavy scent of gardenias. Hunter closed his eyes and let his shoulders slump down. After the last few days of nonstop biking in the hot sun, of trying to escape the Keepers with their scary bows and arrows and chariots, it was so nice to feel safe again, to be able to relax, drift, sink. . . .

Outside the window, bullfrogs throbbed and twanged. Palm fronds rustled in the wind. And then there was the sound of Nana's voice saying, "Everyone happy?" and Mommy replying in a whisper, "Yes, thank you."

Hunter wasn't sure how long he'd been out when he felt a hand on his arm. He opened his eyes. Mommy was standing over him, smiling.

"They're all asleep," she whispered. "Come on."

"Okay." Mommy was so close, Hunter could smell her skin. It smelled salty like the ocean, and powdery and sweet.

Mommy raked her fingers through her hair, which was mussed from lying down with the little ones. She tiptoed through the doorway and into the adjoining bedroom. Hunter tugged on his T-shirt and followed her.

Teacher, Angerman, and Cory were already in bed, although none of them seemed to be asleep. Teacher was in one of the double beds, and Angerman was in the other, just a few feet away. Cory was lying on the big white sofa, still dressed in her gray Confederate soldier's uniform. She was resting her head on a heart-shaped pillow that had words stitched on it: BLESS OUR HOME.

Moonlight spilled through the window. There were candles on the nightstand, flickering and hissing. Nana had told Hunter that she'd made them herself, from bees or honey or something like that. They smelled sweet.

Mommy went over to Teacher's bed and crawled under the covers next to her. Hunter sat down on the edge of the bed next to Angerman and began taking off his shoes. Angerman whispered something to him.

"What was that, Angerman?" Hunter let a shoe thump to the floor and turned around. Angerman was scraping the mannequin's head with the blade of his Swiss Army knife.

"P-pass me a candle, wouldja?" Angerman whispered. "W-we could set him on fire, see if he gives off that b-burning-flesh smell."

Hunter frowned. This guy was really losing it. "Go to sleep, Angerman—and put that knife away before you cut my arm off."

"Prisoner of the United States," Teacher said suddenly. She was sitting up in bed with The Book propped on her lap, unopened. "'member what Baby said? She said, 'Prisoner of the United States.'"

"She was just doing her Baby-talk," Mommy

murmured, nestling under the covers. "It didn't mean anything."

"But what if it *did*?" Teacher went on. She reached over the nightstand and grabbed a piece of paper and a pen. She scribbled some words. "Prisoner . . . of . . . the . . . Yoo-nited . . . States," she said out loud. "What if, okay, what if the president survived Fire-us? And what if he was at this Pisgah Island place when the Keepers took it over? Maybe they took him prisoner. Maybe he's a prisoner there right now."

"No way," Cory said from the couch. "He's probably not even alive anymore. That's what Nana said."

"But he *could* be," Teacher said. "And if he's there, shouldn't we find him and free him from the Keepers?"

Angerman snorted. "Oh, yeah, well, that sounds like a real fun . . . a real f-f-f—" He stopped and began gasping for breath.

"Angerman, you all right?" Mommy bolted straight up.

"F-f-f-fine," Angerman stammered. "F-f-f-fine and d-d-d-dandy!" He let the knife fall to the floor with a clatter.

Mommy and Hunter exchanged a glance. Hunter knew what she was thinking: something was happening to Angerman. He had always been weird and crazy, ever since he joined their family in Lazarus. And it got worse after they ran into the Keepers in Jacksonville.

And now, something *different* was happening. It used to be, you couldn't shut the guy up. He'd go off on one of his newscasts, one of his bizarre long speeches about God or the Civil War or Santa Claus or the weather, and you couldn't make him stop. But all day long today, he'd been stuttering and choking and acting as if he couldn't get his words out, like someone was stuffing a sock down his throat. What was going on?

Cory sat up and swatted a strand of hair out of her eyes. "I think it's way too dangerous," she said. "If Pisgah Island is the same Pisgah where the Keepers live, then that's where Supreme Leader lives. That's where I was going to be sent, if I hadn't come with you guys instead."

"Have you ever met this Supreme Leader dude?" Hunter asked Cory.

"I don't know," Cory said, and looked away. "Maybe once, when I was little, I don't remember."

The flames of the candles licked at the air. Huge shadows wobbled and danced across the sky-blue walls. Cory pulled a thread out of the hem of her military costume and began wrapping it around and around her finger, very tightly.

"We have to think of the twins," Mommy said, frowning at Cory. "If we take them to Pisgah Island, the Keepers'll steal them from us again. And make them go through this Testing, whatever that is."

"Okay, but look," Teacher said. "What if the Fire-us is still out there?"

"Nana said it burned away," Mommy insisted.

"She could be wrong," Teacher replied. "Or maybe it's in a special science lab-ra-tory or something, all locked away. The thing is, if President is still alive, he might have a . . . what doyoucallit . . . an anecdote. We've gotta get that, or else we might all get Fire-us and die anyway. You know, like our First—" Her voice broke, and she turned her head. Mommy curved her body around Teacher's and hugged her.

"I think Teacher's got a point," Hunter spoke up. He hated disagreeing with Mommy, but in this case, he thought Teacher was right. "If the Fire-us is still out there, we've gotta have this ant coat thing. And if there's a chance President is still alive and he's at Pisgah Island, well . . ." He turned and glanced at Angerman, who was lying very still and having some sort of stare-down contest with the mangled mannequin head. "Isn't that why we started this crazy trip to begin with? To find President? Okay, so we're gonna maybe have to deal with the Keepers again. We'll figure out a plan. We'll figure out a good, safe, careful plan that won't put Puppy and Kitty in danger."

Cory unwrapped the string from her finger and threw it on the ground. "Anyone remember what the president's name is?" she said after a moment.

"He was called President letter, something, something," Teacher murmured. "I can't remember."

"For some reason I think of towels when I think of President," Mommy spoke up. "I don't know why."

Angerman began laughing. "President J. J. Pillow-case. President A. K. Washcloth. President B. F. Bedspread. Presi—"

"Angerman," Hunter warned.

Angerman shoved Bad Guy's head in front of Hunter's face. "Hail to the—"

The sound of footsteps interrupted Angerman's rant. In the dim light, Hunter saw Puppy and Kitty standing in the doorway between the two rooms, hand in hand.

Mommy and Cory scrambled to their feet at the same time. Cory got to the twins before Mommy did. "What's the matter, can't sleep?" she murmured.

Puppy shook his head. Kitty meowed. Cory scooped them up in her arms and carried them back through the door. "Come on, I'll tell you this really cool story Ingrid used to tell me when I was a little girl. . . ."

Hunter saw Mommy's shoulders sinking as she turned and crawled back into bed beside Teacher. He knew it was hard for her, letting Cory be a Mommy to the twins when she herself had been their Mommy since Lazarus. But the twins wanted to be with Cory all the time now, ever since they'd found out that she was their *First* Mommy's real-live sister.

No one seemed to want to talk anymore. Hunter took off his other shoe, lay down, and closed his eyes. Beside him, he could feel Angerman's body twitching, could hear him inhaling and exhaling. Hunter was starting to feel scared again—of the prospect of going to Pisgah, of Fire-us that might still be out there somewhere, of exposing Action Figure to more danger . . . even of Angerman lying there next to him, twitching and breathing and being crazy in his head. He tried to think of safe, soothing things . . . the grandmas . . . the nice dinner they'd had tonight . . . the memory of his First Daddy's bright green eyes . . . Mommy's voice as she did bedtime with the little kids.

But none of it made Hunter feel safe or soothed now. He wrapped his arms around his chest and fell into a tense, fitful sleep.

Mommy woke up and blinked into the darkness. It took her a second to remember where she was—*oh, yeah, the Woods*. She groped around in the bed, feeling for Baby and Doll. She always slept with them. And then she remembered that the little kids were in the next room, and had to make herself say out loud, "It's okay, it's okay."

"What?"

Teacher rolled over. Mommy realized that her friend was awake.

"Are you writing dreams, Teacher?" Mommy whispered.

"No, uh-uh. Couldn't sleep."

They lay there side by side, in silence. Their bed was a warm cocoon of sheets and clothes and skin. Outside, night insects whirred and droned and tapped their wings against the mesh screen. One of the goats *maaaaed.* Something, maybe a wild animal, rustled through some nearby bushes, then ran away with quick steps.

All of a sudden Mommy felt a strange wave of pain in her stomach. It felt as though ropes were tugging and pulling at her from inside. "Ow." She moaned.

Teacher sat up. "What is it, Mommy?"

"My stomach. It hurts."

Teacher exhaled sharply. "You're not . . . you're not having a virus, are you? Like Nana was talking about?"

"Don't *say* that!" Mommy cried out. "It's not Fire-us. Or any other kind of virus, either."

"Okay, okay. You want me to find Nana and see if she can give you some medicine?"

"No, I'll be all right. It's just a tummy ache."

From the other bed, Angerman began muttering in his sleep. "Tomorrow expect a high of 90 . . . 100 . . . 110 . . . the thermometer's climbing, climbing, climbing . . ."

"Angerman's having dreams," Mommy whispered to Teacher. "Aren't you going to get The Book and write them down?"

Teacher muttered something.

"What?" Mommy said.

"I don't know if I can," Teacher repeated.

"What do you mean, you don't know if you can? You always write down dreams."

Teacher reached under her pillow, pulled out The Book, and cradled it in her lap, unopened. She traced her fingers over the bumpy cover.

Mommy stared at it, at its thick, creased spine that held their family's history and future together in one place. It was such a holy thing.

Teacher began to speak. "Ever since . . . after we left the Crossroads . . . well, there was this message, and I thought The Book was telling me that I couldn't look at it no more. Like I wasn't allowed to read it."

Mommy sat up and grabbed Teacher's arm. "No, Teacher, that's not true! The Book is so important, you can't stop reading it and writing in it. It's because of The Book that we're all alive. The Book helped us leave Lazarus and come up the river and through the words, I mean woods. And now we're all here in this safe place."

"You think so?" Teacher said in a small voice.

Mommy nodded. "I *know* so. We need The Book. And we need you to read it for us, because nobody else can understand it like you can."

Teacher glanced over at Cory, who was snoring softly on the couch. "You're right. Okay."

Teacher touched the edge of The Book with trembling fingers. Moonlight slanted through the window and illuminated it with a ghostly light.

Mommy had a vague, Before-Time memory of staying up late and reading books under the covers with a flashlight. Shivering, she snuggled closer to Teacher. "Go ahead, open it," she urged.

Teacher hesitated, then opened The Book right to the middle. She gasped.

"What is it, Teacher?" Mommy demanded.

"Mommy! I can read it!"

Mommy squeezed her arm. "Good! What does it say?"

"'Back-to-school specials all day Saturday extended shopping hours,'" Teacher read.

"That's wonderful," Mommy said, smiling. "That's really wonderful."

Chapter Five

Cory awoke early, hearing something tap . . . tap-tap, click nearby. She turned her head to look out the window and saw a small goat standing up on its hind legs, its cloven front hooves propped against the windowsill while it stretched to nibble at a bush. Its hooves made delicate clicks and taps against the glass as it jerked at the leaves, and the twiggy tip of the branch clicked against the window, too. Bite, jerk, tap, click, nibble, chew. The goat looked straight at Cory as it ate: the pupils of its yellow eyes were like vertical slits, and the nubbly bumps that would soon be horns looked scaly and rough.

And I beheld another beast coming up out of the earth; and he had two horns like a lamb, and he spake as a dragon. From her memory came the voice of Deuteronomy 29:28, the leader and minister of the Keepers back at the Crossroads, where she had lived for so long. The goat kept its demonic stare upon her as it chewed, little bits of green poking out from the corners of its mouth. Cory had to look away.

She couldn't bear the thought of being with the Keepers again. She could tell the others wanted to go to Pisgah Island, but it had to be full of Keepers. That was where the Supreme Leader was—she had heard it mentioned many times. "Send word to Pisgah," or "Awaiting instructions from Pisgah," were so commonly said at the Crossroads it was as though Pisgah were a crystal ball that gave answers to all questions. No, she couldn't bear the thought of going to Pisgah.

But ever since her Visioning, she had been searching for her path. So far, her path had been with Mommy and Hunter and the others, to look after Puppy and Kitty and keep them safe. So maybe she would have to go to Pisgah, if the others decided to.

On the other hand, she had turned her back on the Keepers and everything about them, so maybe she should ignore the whole Visioning thing. Since none of the others knew what she was talking about whenever she mentioned her Visioning, she was pretty sure that it was something the Keepers had invented. If she was leaving her old life behind, if she was sure it had all been an evil sham, then perhaps her Visioning was, too. Maybe there was no path. Maybe she should just take Puppy and Kitty and strike out on her own.

A soft groan from the bed across the room broke into Cory's troubled thoughts. She pushed herself up onto her elbows. "Mommy?" she called in a soft voice.

Mommy let out a jaw-cracking yawn. "I was having the weirdest dream," she murmured. "I was driving a chariot but instead of a horse it was pulled by goats. And they were so stubborn they would never go where I wanted them to. So I couldn't go anywhere."

"I think they look a little bit—" Cory hesitated to use the word *evil*, which had such an ominous meaning. "Creepy. A little bit scary. Like they can read your mind."

"If they can read my mind all they'll find out is I'm hungry," Mommy whispered, smiling. She began to push the covers away, trying not to disturb Teacher, who was still dead to the world beside her with her head under a pillow.

From across the room, Cory saw Mommy's smile freeze. Mommy was staring down at her legs. "What?" Cory asked. "What's wrong?"

When Mommy didn't answer, Cory flung her own covers back and crossed the room in three strides to Mommy's side. "What—oh." She broke off, her own face flushing scarlet.

"Something's wrong!" Mommy gasped, looking horror-struck. The lap of her nightgown and the sheet beneath her were spotted and smeared vivid red.

"No, it's just—" Cory patted Mommy's shoulder in an awkward gesture of comfort. "That's what Nana was talking about. She had a special name for it that I don't remember, but it's the Curse. Girls all get it when they—"

"What's going on?" came Teacher's cracked and creaky voice from beneath her pillow. She pushed herself up and brushed the hair away from her eyes. There was a wrinkly-looking crease on one cheek.

"I'm bleeding, Teacher!" Mommy said. "I'm sick—maybe I got the Fire-us—what about Baby and Doll and—"

"Shh!" Cory hissed as Mommy's voice rose in panic.

In the other bed, the boys began to stir.

"G'morning," Hunter said to the ceiling. Angerman let out a muffled grunt and kicked in his sleep.

Hunter reached out to feel for his glasses and found them on the table beside the bed. The girls all stared at him, and then Cory tried to block Mommy from view as Hunter sat upright. But Mommy was struggling wildly to shove the covers away, trying to see how much blood there was. She was also beginning to cry.

"Hey, whassamatter?" Hunter asked.

"Nothing!" Cory said. "Just—we need Nana, okay? Could you go get Nana?"

"Sure, but what's the—"

"Just go get her!" Cory cried.

Teacher was completely awake, and trying to lift Mommy's nightgown to see where the blood was coming from. "What happened? Did you cut yourself?"

Cory threw her hands up and shook her head. It figured that kids who raised themselves wouldn't know anything about that kind of stuff. And she wasn't going to be the one to explain it. She'd leave that job to Nana.

Hunter walked out to the patio in a daze, almost bumping into a goat before it shied away from him with a petulant bleat. The "talk" that Nana had just given to him and Angerman had left him with a very peculiar feeling, like he was partway out of his own body. Behind him, the door slid shut as Angerman followed him out. They sat without speaking on the cracked cement wall and stared at their sneakers. Some of Nana's words came back to Hunter like disjointed echoes: *with blood . . . egg . . . baby begins to grow.*

"Wow," Hunter said at last.

Angerman didn't reply.

"I guess Mommy . . . I mean, she could . . ." Hunter trailed off as a sudden wave of heat washed over him and left his skin prickling.

"Hunter!" A lady's voice wafted around the corner of the building.

He leaped to his feet, desperate for something to do,

to occupy his thoughts and crowd out what Nana had told him. Trotting, he reached the driveway and found Kirsten standing beside a golf cart. "What is it?" he asked.

"Listen, dear, take a golf cart. There's a drugstore down the highway," Kirsten began, turning him by the shoulder and pointing to the access road of the Woods. "We've cleaned it out of most of the stuff we needed, but Mommy—it's funny to call her that, isn't it? Doesn't she have a real name either?"

"What about Mommy?" Hunter asked with that partway-out-of-his-own-body sensation again.

"Mommy needs something from the drugstore, Hunter," Kirsten explained. "The signs are still up in the aisles, I think, or at least they were last time I was there. Look for a sign that says 'feminine products,' and get a box from that aisle."

Hunter gave her a dubious look. "A box of what?"

Kirsten let out a chuckle. "Tampons, sweetheart."

There was a thick lump in Hunter's throat. He had a very bad feeling about this errand. "W-what do they look like?"

"Well, sort of—" Kirsten paused, frowning. "Well, they don't actually put a *picture* of them on the box, as I recall. Just look for the word, *tampon*. T-A-M—"

"I know how to spell," Hunter broke in. "I've seen those boxes. I just didn't know what . . . what it . . . what they were for. . . ."

In fact, he still wasn't entirely clear, but he was quite sure he didn't want anyone to explain it to him. He took a reluctant step toward the golf cart.

"Can't you go?" he asked, looking back at the white-haired woman.

Kirsten smiled and shook her head. "You poor thing. I would, but I have to help with breakfast. Go on now. Take a left at the end of the driveway and keep going until you come to the strip mall and you'll see the Right-Drug 24-Hour Store. The sooner the better. Mommy needs—"

"OKAY!" Hunter jumped into the driver's seat and switched on the motor before Kirsten could say anything more. He struggled with the lever to make the cart go backward, and missed bashing into another golf cart by a goat's whisker. Blushing from head to toe, Hunter reversed, turned, and then tore down the driveway, scattering gravel as he went.

Teacher sat on the vinyl couch, the backs of her legs sticking to the shiny upholstery. The Book was spread open in her lap, and Teddy Bear and Doll sat on either side of her, looking at the open pages.

"Cold. Your. Child. Be. A. Model," Doll read with painstaking slowness.

"Could. That word is *could*," Teacher corrected her. "Very good, Doll. You try one, Teddy."

She liked doing School with the children. It was safe and familiar and reminded her of the old days in Lazarus. Before everything began to change—the way they lived, their plans, even their bodies. Teacher snuck a glance at Mommy from under her lashes. Nana's explanation had been as shocking to them as if she had said Mommy was coming down with Fire-us. Why blood? Whose idea was *that*?

The examining room door slammed open, and Action Figure burst out into the waiting area. "Not sick!" he crowed, karate-kicking an imaginary foe.

Teacher looked beyond him at Nana, who stood in the doorway of her doctor's office, wearing a white coat and with a sort of Y-shaped tube hanging around her neck. The office and waiting room were down at the end of one of the long corridors of the retirement home complex. Nana was giving them all physical exams.

"Hey, that's good, Action," Cory said. "You're all better."

"No more sick," the boy repeated with another karate kick at an empty chair.

"How long was he sick for?" Nana asked. She pulled the rubbery tube thing from around her neck and began fiddling with it.

Mommy looked up from the magazine she was reading. "For a few days he had a jar of some stuff called Man Power and he was eating it, but it had some kind of mold growing in it and it made him sick."

"Why was he eating it at all?" Nana asked.

"He wanted to grow up," Cory explained, "and be a man."

Teacher saw Mommy blush and lower her face further over her magazine.

"Who's next?" Nana asked.

Teacher peeled herself off the couch, snapping The Book closed. "I guess I'm last. There's lots of magazines to practice reading with," she told Teddy Bear and Doll. She almost always carried The Book with her, and she certainly wouldn't leave it with the children.

Once she was sure they were busy with something to read, she followed Nana into the doctor's office. She could almost remember another office like this—the white countertop, the high padded table you had to climb a footstool to sit on, the chair on wheels. Nana put the forked ends of the tube into her ears and held up the disk on the end.

"Put your book down on the table, dear, I need to listen to your heart."

Teacher set The Book aside, but kept one hand on it as Nana held the end with the metal disk, to Teacher's chest.

"Breathe in, nice deep breath," Nana said.

The disk was cool, and Teacher breathed in and then out in a long sigh. It was so nice to have a Grown-up—a good, safe Grown-up—taking charge and taking care of them. Nana was a doctor. She was smart and knew how to do things. Teacher sighed another long, contented breath, smiling at the wall. A real doctor had examined all of them.

"What's wrong with Angerman?" Teacher asked. "Is he sick? He's getting worse and worse all the time."

Nana took Teacher's chin and turned her to face the bright window. Then she pulled down on Teacher's chin to open her mouth. "Say ahhh," Nana ordered. "Angerman is as healthy as the rest of you are, in his body. But people can get hurt inside their heads."

Teacher's tongue was getting dried out. She made some spit and swallowed, moistening her mouth as Nana looked into her ears. "Can he get better?"

"I don't know." Nana pulled up the rolling chair and sat in front of Teacher, feeling her shins and ankles, pressing Teacher's kneecaps. She frowned as she continued. "If something terrible happened—not that the end of the world isn't terrible enough, lord knows—but if Angerman saw something that was especially shocking to him, then he might have decided to switch off reality. It's not so surprising, really. What is surprising is that we aren't all crazy."

"I'm not crazy," Teacher said, inching The Book a little closer to her.

Nana smiled at her and hitched one thumb over her shoulder. "You can get down, now. No, you're not crazy, dear. You kids are amazingly healthy, all things considered. You've been very smart to take care of yourselves so well."

"Mommy always made us brush our teeth and take vitamins and eat good food instead of just candy," Teacher explained, reaching for The Book. "It's all here. I wrote it all down."

As she tucked The Book under her arm, she noticed a photograph on the wall. It was a black-and-white picture of a handsome man with dark, curly hair, standing in front of a desk in a fancy room with flags. The carpet at his feet had a circle with an eagle in the middle of it and some writing around the perimeter. Someone had written over the picture in black marker: *Happy 100th Birthday to Belinda Graham.* Teacher took a step closer, scrutinizing the photo.

The writing on the carpet at the man's feet said *Seal of the President of the United States of America.*

"Who's this?" Teacher asked.

Nana clicked a pen and made some notes on a clipboard. She glanced up. "Who, Belinda? She was my aunt—my mother's eldest sister. She passed away three—no, four years ago. She turned one hundred two months before the outbreak so she got her picture. My mother is still with us. She lives here. Gladys. You met her. Mrs. Johnson."

Teacher nodded, recalling the frail and cloudy-eyed lady who acted so dreamy and said nonsense things. But she wasn't really interested in Nana's family history. She looked back over her shoulder at the doctor.

"In the picture," she said. "Who is it in the picture?"

Arching her eyebrows in surprise, Nana said, "I thought you knew."

"Knew what?"

"But you've been traveling all this time to look for him," Nana said in a puzzled voice. "It's the president. The last one we ever had. President J. Colin McDowell."

Teacher knew that if Nana had had that listening tube on her just then, she would have heard Teacher's heart give a violent thud and then begin to pound at a furious pace. She glanced back at Nana again. The doctor was busy looking for something in a drawer, so her back was turned.

In a heartbeat, Teacher unhooked the framed photo from the wall and stuck it between the thick pages of her scrapbook.

"Okay, see you later," Teacher said, and hurried out of the room.

Chapter Six

Angerman lay back in the long plastic chair and closed his eyes against the bright sun. His eyelids swam with color: orange, red, and black all mixed up, like fire. He shook his head back and forth very fast. Then he sat still and tried to focus on the tiny black dots. It was a game he used to play as a kid. Even back then, the tiny black dots used to drive him crazy. One would float and bob across his field of vision, then disappear; and then another, identical one would start floating and bobbing, at the same pace.

Ever see those dots when you close your eyes? he had once asked Sam.

They're bugs that live in your brain, Sam had replied, laughing.

The *thwunk* of a tennis ball broke into Angerman's thoughts. He jerked upright, and his eyelids flew open.

"Angerman, git it! Git the ball!" Baby screeched.

Angerman blinked. Baby was standing in the middle of the tennis court, waving a silver racquet at him. At least he *thought* it was a tennis court. Crackly green asphalt, the ghostly vestiges of stripes, a sagging net with giant holes. He remembered tennis courts from the Before Time, and the words *deuce* and *your ad* and *love. Love?*

"Angermaaaaaaaan! The *ball*!" Baby's voice was all impatience now. Sunlight winked off her blond hair and off the silver rim of her racquet.

Angerman glanced down and saw that a yellow ball was rolling back and forth, back and forth under his chair. He picked it up and fingered the peach-fuzzy texture of it, then threw it in Baby's direction, hard.

His aim was way off. The ball veered to the right of Baby, who nevertheless let out a shrill cry and chased after it with her racquet. The other little kids did the same, laughing and yelling. The ball landed near a tall tuft of weeds that had sprouted through a crack in the asphalt. Overhead, a seagull swooped through the hot air and shrieked. The sound fell over Angerman like pieces of broken glass.

Action Figure got to the ball first and began whacking it with his tennis racquet. "Die, bam-bam!" he cried out.

Kitty ran to catch up with the others, pumping her thin brown arms, but her foot caught on a dead branch, and she went sprawling to the ground. She didn't make a sound but began trying to hoist herself up.

The other kids were busy cheering Action Figure on and had their backs to her.

Someone help Kitty get up! Angerman tried to shout. But nothing came out of his mouth. He tried to draw breath, sweating with alarm.

Ever see a dead cat lying in the road? Bad Guy chuckled. His eyes were staring at Angerman over the rim of his backpack, which he had tossed to the ground next to someone's old towel with the initials CLB on it.

"Shut . . . *up*!"

Angerman started to get up out of his chair, then staggered back down again. His head swam with heat and dizziness. At the same moment Kitty scrambled to her feet and rubbed her palms against her pale blue cotton dress that Doll had belted with a man's tie and an old pair of panty hose. She skipped off toward the others.

Nobody's interested in your opinion, boy, Bad Guy told him.

Angerman tried to say something, but his voice came out in a high squeak. His eyes felt as though they were bugging out of his head. What was happening to him? Had Bad Guy completely taken over his brain? Why couldn't he talk anymore?

Nana had asked him a bunch of questions during his physical this morning, but he hadn't been able to answer any of them.

What's your name, dear?

Does it hurt when I touch you here?

Do you feel any scratchiness in your throat?

Where do you come from?

Do you ever hear ringing in your ears?

Did you have a lot of family, before?

Do you have trouble sleeping?

Do you know where you are?

How many fingers am I holding up?

Do you know who I am?

Nearby, on the other side of the fence, a couple of the goats were munching on grass. They smelled oily, bad. Angerman hated their smell. And he hated their eyes, too, the thin black pupils against the yellow irises. They watched Action Figure and the others while they ate.

Just beyond the goats, Angerman saw the old lady Kirsten strolling with Teacher, Cory, and Hunter through the grandmas' vegetable garden. Every few minutes Kirsten bent down very slowly, one hand on her back, and plucked something out of the ground: a dirt-covered carrot, a plume of lettuce. Cory held out a basket, and Kirsten dropped the vegetables into it.

Angerman frowned. They seemed to be having a fine old time without him. They always had a fine old time without him, especially these days.

But where was Mommy? Angerman hadn't seen her since this morning, since the business with the blood. Nana had explained all that to him and Hunter, but he had missed half of what she said. Bad Guy had been talking up a storm, hissing in his ear—stuff about *handmaids* and *brides* and the *New Savior*. Angerman had caught some of Nana's speech, though—something about Mommy being a woman now, and Angerman and Hunter having deep voices and hair on their faces and perms. Or was it *sperms*? But what did it all mean? Maybe Teacher could look it up in The Book.

The goats scurried off suddenly, their hooves rustling through the grass. Angerman glanced at them. They ran toward the main house and disappeared around the corner.

Angerman heard more rustling, then snorting. What was that? Another goat? He put his hands over his eyes and turned his head to the left, then to the right.

Almost immediately, he spotted the beast. It was coming through the overgrown oleander bushes on the other side of the tennis court. It was enormous and brown, with tiny black eyes and two thin tusks that curved out of its snout like knives.

This just in! Today, residents of the Woods were paid

an unexpected visit by a wild boar. When asked if he planned to dress up in one of the grandmas' outfits and wait around for some little girl to come sit on his lap, he replied that no, he preferred instead to go for the big prize! A tennis court full of unsuspecting children! The more the merrier.

Angerman leaped to his feet to scream at Teddy Bear and Puppy and Kitty and the others. But his throat tightened up, and nothing came out. In the meantime, the boar was trotting toward an opening in the fence. In moments, it would reach the kids, who were happily whacking at the tennis ball with their racquets.

"Somebody, help!" Angerman squeaked.

But nobody heard. Angerman glanced around, his heart thudding in his chest. Kirsten, Hunter, Teacher, and Cory were off in the vegetable garden, oblivious. How could he get their attention in time? And even if he could, what would they do? The boar was enormous, twice as big as any of them. Three times, even.

Time, time, time for a bar-bee-que! Bad Guy giggled.

Without thinking, Angerman reached down and yanked Bad Guy out of his backpack.

Hey, what're you doing, boy? Bad Guy demanded. *Heyyyyy!*

Angerman lifted Bad Guy over his head, then flung him at one of the windows of the main house. This time, his aim was perfect. The window broke with a loud crash, and shards of glass flew everywhere.

"What was that?" Angerman heard Doll cry out. "Mommy!"

Excited by the noise, the boar began to charge. Teddy Bear saw it as he turned, and he began to scream in terror. Seconds later, Nana burst out of the house, methodically loading bullets into a silver pistol. She stopped at the edge of the tennis court, aimed the pistol at the boar, and fired.

The boar let out a loud squeal, or the children did—Angerman's head was throbbing as though someone had hit him. Nana fired again, and the boar crumpled to the ground. It kicked and shuddered, then lay still. Blood bubbled out between its eyes and turned the green grass red.

There was a stunned silence, the children horror-struck and frozen in place. Then Action Figure let out a wild whoop. "Kilt it!" he shouted, waving his tennis racquet. "Die, bam-bam! Whoo-hoo!"

Teacher, Cory, and Hunter rushed, breathless, to the tennis court. "What happened?" Cory yelled, clutching Puppy and Kitty to her chest.

Nana turned to Angerman. "Thanks for letting me know," she said in a grim voice. Then she hurried over to Teddy Bear, Doll, and Baby, who were huddled in the middle of the tennis court and whimpering in fear at the huge dead bloody thing.

Mommy pulled her knees to her chest and stared up at the full moon rising over the ocean as the day lingered in the sky. She dug tiny pits into the ground with her bare toes, and felt the cool clamminess of the sand below. A wave rolled toward her feet, then hesitated, then rolled away from her, leaving a line of frothing white bubbles.

Baby and Doll sat on either side of her, snuggling into her and sucking their thumbs. She knew they were still shaken up from the boar incident. She had been in the big kids' room at the time, taking a nap, trying to get over her bad stomachache from the men-thing Nana had told her about. Since then, Mommy had heard all about the boar from each of the little kids, who had told wildly different versions of the same story, and from Nana. Angerman, who had been there, too, hadn't said a word about it. Of course, he wasn't talking about much of *anything* lately.

"Mommy! Bar-bee-que!"

Mommy glanced up and saw Teddy Bear smiling and waving at her. She smiled and waved back. The air was thick with the smell of roasting meat. Nana had concocted some sort of gizmo—a pit or a spit, or something like that. The boar, which Nana and Hunter had skinned, was turning around and around on a metal pole. Its juices kept dripping into the fire and making the flames hiss and crackle.

"Mrs. Johnson, time for supper."

"Doctor told me I couldn't eat steak because of my bad arteries."

"Can I make you a plate, Nellie?"

"My, doesn't that smell delicious!"

The voices of the grandmas drifted to Mommy over the crackling flames. She still wasn't used to the sound of Grown-ups after all these years. She tugged her dress over her knees, stood up, and held out her hands. "Come on, girls, time to eat."

"'kay."

"'kay, Mommy."

Baby and Doll jumped to their feet. The three of them walked over to the spit. Nana was slicing big wedges of meat and slapping them onto plates, which

Kirsten handed to her.

Mommy stared at the boar, at the crusty brown surface of it where its dark juices bubbled and mingled with red blood. She felt vaguely sick.

Hunter and Action Figure were standing nearby. Mommy stole a glance at Hunter. She could tell that he knew she was there, but he wouldn't look at her. In fact, he hadn't looked at her all day.

Off in the distance, Angerman sat alone on a piece of driftwood and moved his lips at the scarred and mutilated mannequin head, which was lying in the sand. Angerman had crowned it with wet clumps of greenish-black seaweed. Cory was herding Puppy and Kitty toward the food.

Action Figure took a plate from Kirsten. Ignoring the fork and knife she also gave him, he began eating the meat with his bare hands. "Mmm, mmm, good!" he announced.

"Super-duper!" Teddy Bear agreed.

The other little kids began crowding around the spit and clamoring for plates. "Okay, one at a time. There's enough for everyone," Nana said, laughing.

Mommy waited till last to get her plate, saw that all the little kids were settled in their spots with various grandmas, then went off to join Teacher. The older girl was sitting a little way away from the others, poring over The Book.

"Aren't you gonna eat?" Mommy called out to her.

"I found something, Mommy!" Teacher leaned over The Book with an eager expression.

Mommy transferred her plate from one hand to the other and sat down carefully beside Teacher. In the firelight, the thick and rippled pages of The Book looked especially ghostly. She tried not to stare at the words or pictures on them. That was Teacher's job. Although it was tempting, sometimes. Out of the corner of her eye, Mommy caught sight of a shiny magazine picture, of a smiling First Mommy holding a baby in her arms. She wished she knew what it signified.

"What does The Book say, Teacher?"

Teacher took a deep breath, then said, "'Breast-feeding isn't always best.'"

Hearing the word *breast*, Mommy remembered the talk Nana had given Teacher and her this morning. She could feel her cheeks flushing. "W-what does that mean?" she stammered at Teacher.

Teacher pointed to the other page. "And over here, The Book gives us the holy messages, 'The best car warranty your money can buy!' and 'Georgia is for lovers.' I think all these things are connected."

Mommy nodded. She moved her food around with her fork but didn't eat it.

Across the stretch of sandy beach, the crackling flames cast a golden glow over the grandmas and the little kids and Cory. Everyone was eating and talking and laughing. Action Figure was acting out a story for two of the grandmas. Mommy guessed that it was the story of the wild boar, coming toward the little kids on the tennis court.

Two ovals of light gleamed at her from across the fire. Mommy realized with a start that Hunter was staring at her from behind his glasses.

He jerked his head around abruptly. "Everyone got their food?" he snapped at Nana.

Teacher was saying something about The Book, but Mommy wasn't listening. She was filled with a deep well of sadness, because everything was different now. She touched her stomach, at the place that hurt, and listened to its answering grumble. It was time to eat. She picked up her fork and speared a piece of the meat and lifted it to her mouth, tasting the blood.

Chapter Seven

Cory lay on her back, staring up at the dark. She could still smell the smoke of the bonfire that clung to her worn gray uniform, still taste the grease and gravy of the roasted pig in the corners of her mouth, still feel the tension that had crackled in the air like sparks between Mommy and the boys—both at the cookout and again when they'd gone separate ways for bedtime.

Now she could hear Mommy and Teacher whispering together in bed. They still shared a bed, even though the boys were in another room now. Cory had the other bed to herself, although Puppy and Kitty were sleeping beside it in a nest of blankets—the way they preferred.

"I think somebody should go see," came Teacher's voice, husky with tiredness. "What if he is there, and he's a prisoner?"

"Nana says he probably isn't alive," Mommy replied. The bedsprings squeaked as she shifted. "I say we just stay here where it's safe."

There was a pause in the darkness. Then Teacher said, "Hunter thinks we should look."

There was another long pause. Cory held her breath, waiting to hear what Mommy would say. As far as she could tell, Mommy and Hunter hadn't even looked at each other all day, let alone exchanged words. Every time they found themselves in the same room, one of them would beat a sudden retreat. At last, Mommy let out a tiny sigh.

"He told you that?"

"Yeah, and it's hard to tell, but I think Angerman—"

"We *should* go," Cory broke in. "I've been thinking about it, and I think we *should* go and see."

The springs of the other bed creaked again as both girls turned toward her in the dark. Cory could just barely make out the sheen of their eyes reflecting some stray light. "You're awake?" Teacher asked.

"Yeah, and I think we should go. The whole idea was to find this president guy, and if there's a chance he's there, we should go see."

"But, Cory—" Mommy began.

There was a fumbling noise, and then a click and the beam of a flashlight shot up toward the ceiling. A small flurry of movement on the walls and a tiny clicking sound told Cory that palmetto bugs or cockroaches were fleeing the brightness. As her eyes adjusted, Cory saw Mommy set the flashlight on end and sit up in the bed to look at her.

"Cory, there might be someone there who knows you."

There was an uncomfortable thump behind Cory's ribs. She lifted her chin in a show of defiance. "I thought of that."

"They might have heard you ran away." Teacher's face loomed pale as a ghost behind the flashlight's beam. "They might be really . . . mad at you. It could be dangerous."

"I thought of that, too," Cory said, trying to ignore

the way her heart bumped in her chest. "But if you guys go, I'm going with you."

"No, Cory, someone will see you—your hair—you don't look like other girls," Mommy said with fear in her voice.

Cory swung her legs off the bed and padded across the room. Angerman's Swiss Army knife was sitting on a shelf. She had seen it that afternoon and had used it to clean the dirt out from under her fingernails. Now she pried open the blade and grabbed her thick blond braid in one hand.

"What are you doing!" Mommy gasped.

A muffled rustling came from beside the bed, and Cory looked to see two small faces peering at her over the edge. Puppy and Kitty stared at her without speaking.

"Getting a haircut," Cory said, giving the two little ones a confident smile. Then she began sawing at her braid, wincing a bit as individual hairs pulled and pinched her scalp. Cory worked the knife back and forth, the blade making a soft ripping sound against her hair, until at last the thick plait came free and lay across her open palm like a frayed length of rope. "I bet there's some scissors around here, too, and I can get it even shorter."

The others were silent and wide-eyed. Cory stood looking at the braid in her hand and felt the faintest pang of regret. Then she caught sight of her reflection in the window, which showed black against the night sky. In her Civil War uniform, with short hair, she looked like the ghost of a tall young soldier.

With a lopsided smile, she jabbed the knife point first

onto the windowsill and turned away while it was still quivering.

The morning dawned clear and breezy, and Teacher was having no luck at all rounding up the little kids for School after breakfast. They wanted to play outside with the baby goats and make daisy chains and dig holes in the tennis court, and they kept running away from her with shrieks and giggles.

"You have to do School," Teacher said, hands on her hips and a stern expression on her face. "This isn't vacation."

Teddy Bear ran by her and dodged away just before she could grab him. It didn't seem right to her to chase after them—The Book was too dignified for that, and she didn't like to put it down on the grass in case a goat went for it. Just before breakfast, a goat had walked into the sunroom and started nibbling an old magazine that one of the ladies had left on a chair. Teacher wasn't taking any chances with her precious scrapbook.

Exasperated, she stalked indoors and slumped in a chair beside Mrs. Johnson, who was smiling serenely into space. Teacher remembered Nana saying that Mrs. Johnson was her mother. It was funny to think of someone as old as Nana having her mother still, when nobody else did. For a moment, Teacher sat glaring out the window, watching the children romping barefoot. As she watched, Action Figure skidded through a pile of fresh goat droppings and landed on his behind. He started laughing so hard he couldn't stand up again.

"So I told him I wouldn't pay for it, because I hadn't ordered it, but he was so insistent," Mrs. Johnson spoke up suddenly. "I didn't like it at all."

Teacher looked over, trying to be polite. "Really? I'm sorry. I hope it won't happen again."

"It's not your fault, dear," Mrs. Johnson said, her cloudy eyes crinkling up at the corners. She reached out to pat Teacher's hand, and then left her hand on Teacher's. Her skin felt cool and papery.

"It's just that I didn't order it," she repeated. "And so it didn't seem fair to make me pay for it, that's all."

Teacher kept smiling, but she wasn't sure Mrs. Johnson was talking to her or what the woman was talking about. She didn't want to pull her hand away though. That wouldn't be Manners. While Teacher sat wondering how to get away without hurting the old lady's feelings, Mommy walked in and stood gazing out the window.

"Did you need me to help you?" Teacher spoke up in a loud voice and giving Mommy a hopeful look.

"Huh?" Mommy turned around, clearly puzzled.

Teacher jerked her head slightly toward Mrs. Johnson, trying to communicate to Mommy that she needed a polite exit. But Mommy seemed distracted and didn't understand.

"No, I'm not really doing anything," Mommy said, turning back to the window.

"Lisa, Lisa, Lisa," Mrs. Johnson said with a sorry shake of her head. She looked at Teacher. "I wish you hadn't given up ballet lessons. By the way, is David still here?"

Teacher wondered what to do. The old lady was clearly lost in a fog of old memories, confused about where she was. She chewed a little dry skin off her lower lip. Maybe the kindest thing would simply be to go along with it. "David?" she asked.

"Such a beautiful child. I remember seeing him once in a while when they all came down for vacations," the woman said. She let out a sigh. "Those were happy days, weren't they?"

"Sure," Teacher said, casting a desperate look toward Mommy.

Mrs. Johnson wrapped her brittle fingers around Teacher's hand and leaned forward, smiling. "I was so surprised to see him when he came the other day. Right out of the blue, there he is! Of course, he's taller now."

Mommy left the window and came to sit on Mrs. Johnson's other side. "Who is?"

The woman's head shook slightly as she turned. "Oh? What's that? David, dear. David—David— Now what was their last name?"

Teacher and Mommy exchanged a look and Teacher shrugged. Mrs. Johnson was obviously thinking of some kid she used to know and now was all mixed up about it because of the All Zymers. "He's not here anymore," Teacher said.

Mrs. Johnson's happy, bright expression faded. She frowned and drew a dozen wrinkles into her forehead. "But I thought—"

At once, she beamed again. "There. He is still here," she said, and raised a trembling hand to point out the window.

Teacher and Mommy both craned their necks to see what the old woman was pointing at, and at the same time, they both stifled a laugh. Angerman was pacing back and forth across the lawn, waving his arms in the air and muttering to himself.

"That's Angerman, Mrs. Johnson," Mommy said in a gentle voice. "He came with us, remember?"

"But, Lisa," Mrs. Johnson began, turning to look at Teacher. "Lisa, don't you remember we used to talk about what a handsome child he was?"

"Well . . . sure," Teacher said, glancing at Mommy and then giving Mrs. Johnson a comforting pat on the shoulder. "Sure I do. I just forgot, that's all."

"The whole family. All of them, so attractive, so charming! Ah . . . I suppose they'll be coming for Thanksgiving, like they always do. We're going to have such a nice turkey this year for Thanksgiving, and I promised to make my famous candied yams. Everybody always asks me to make them." Beaming, Mrs. Johnson folded her hands in her lap and let out another reminiscent sigh. She nodded, and her smile faded, and even as the girls watched, it seemed as if the old lady retreated far away into the fog of her befuddled memories.

Carefully, quietly, Teacher and Mommy rose from their chairs and tiptoed out of the room.

"Poor old lady," Mommy whispered.

Teacher paused in the doorway and looked back, pressing the comforting weight of The Book against her hip. The old woman had retreated into sunny memories and was turning the pages like a scrapbook, reminiscing about the good old days of the Before Time.

"Maybe she's happier this way," she said, and a sudden shiver raised the hair on her arms. "She doesn't even know all those things are gone forever."

* * *

Lunch that day was shredded leftover pork, mixed with goat cheese and chopped onions and herbs from Kirsten's vegetable garden. Sitting at the big table in the kitchen, Hunter shoveled huge forkfuls into his mouth, savoring every bite of the fresh meat. It was so good. He couldn't remember anything ever tasting so good. Beside him, Action Figure was eating with his hands and reenacting the boar attack, while Nana chopped meat finer and mixed it with milk for the oldest ladies to eat.

"Pig 'as gonna bite Kitty, but I shotum with my bone arra," the boy boasted as little bits of pork fell from his overstuffed mouth. He gulped and swallowed, and grinned a huge, greasy grin. "Kiltit."

"You don't even have your bone arrows no more," Baby protested. "Liar, liar, pants on fire."

"KILTIT!" Action Figure roared. He climbed up onto his chair and stood on it, pointing a sticky finger at Baby. "Baby! You baby!"

"Okay, settle down," Mommy said with a warning look. "Sit in your seat and do Manners, Action. Or you don't get any more pig meat," she added when he held his ground.

At that, Action Figure dropped down and sat with his knees folded up against the table in front of him. He grabbed another fistful of pork. He said no more as he licked it off his fingers.

"Well! You certainly know how to handle *him*," Nana said with a laugh as she reached for another slab of meat to chop up.

Hunter glanced at Mommy, and then away again before she could catch his eyes. He pushed his plate away and put his elbows on the table. "Nana, we've been talking—some of us—" he added, wondering if Mommy was looking at him. "And we want to go over to Pisgah Island and check it out. See if the prisoner—I mean the president—is there or not."

Nana pushed a wisp of gray hair from her forehead with the back of her hand, slowly shaking her head. Hunter waited, just to be polite. It didn't really matter what she said. She couldn't stop them.

"If you're determined to go, there's nothing I can do about it other than to ask you to please hurry back," Nana said at last.

Angerman let out a grunt, and everyone turned to him to see if he was actually going to say something. But he didn't. He just kept his head down, nibbling on a frond of parsley. From a certain angle, it almost looked to Hunter as though Angerman had been crying. But then Angerman tipped his face down even further, and Hunter couldn't tell. He had a sudden ripple of apprehension that Angerman shouldn't go with them.

"I also think you should leave the younger children here," Nana continued, looking around at the little ones. Teddy Bear noticed he was being discussed and stared with his open mouth full of food.

"Psst," Teacher whispered to her little brother, and made a ferocious chewing motion with her mouth.

Teddy Bear began chewing and swallowed hard.

"We pretty much figured that anyway," Cory spoke up. She gestured toward Puppy and Kitty with her fork. "I'm not letting them anywhere near the Keepers again."

Hunter was amazed again, just as he had been when he'd seen her for the first time this morning. Cory looked so different with her hair cut short—even her voice sounded different. Deeper. Harder. Something. Anyone who knew she was a girl could see she was, but someone who wasn't expecting to see a girl there might think she was a boy. He had a fuzzy memory of a picture in a book of a brave-eyed young man and a Grown-up voice saying *crews-hating night*. But he didn't know what *night* had to do with the picture, which was lit with beams of light coming down from behind a cloud, and he didn't know why the crews would hate the night, anyway. He didn't even know how he could remember a strange phrase like that. He shook his head.

"Can we take two of the golf carts?" Hunter asked, turning back to Nana. "It'll be faster."

"Of course, but bear in mind, they don't go very far or very fast on a single charge. You'll have to stop fairly often in full sun and let them juice up again. And take plenty of drinking water—you can't be sure of finding good water as you go up the coast."

Hunter hesitated for a moment, and then blurted out. "And can we take the gun?"

Nana turned on him with a hawkish look. "*What?*"

"For protection," he said, swallowing hard. "We might run into another boar or a panther or something—on the way."

"Absolutely not," Nana said, chopping the meat even finer with the big knife. "Guns and children do not go together under any circumstances. I'm a doctor, and I've seen what happens when kids get their hands on guns."

Hunter flushed. "But we're not kids," he muttered.

"You're not taking it, and that's final. You see a panther or a boar, just put the pedal to the metal and drive away from it—it'll be scared of the golf cart, believe me."

There was an uncomfortable silence. Hunter ate a mouthful of pork, trying hard not to let his frustration show. He was a little afraid of the gun, anyway, and was almost glad she wouldn't let them take it. But it still hurt his pride that she didn't think he could handle it.

"Do you have a map?" Teacher asked.

"Oh, sure," Nana said, her voice easier now that the subject of guns was out of the way. "We've got atlases, road maps. It shouldn't be hard at all to find the place. As long as the roads aren't washed out."

Hunter speared another piece of meat with his fork. "Don't worry. We've dealt with worse things than washed-out roads," he said. "We'll get there."

Chapter Eight

Angerman stood under the draping arm of the banyan tree and adjusted his shades. He'd found them in one of the bedrooms last night on top of a dresser next to a brown pill bottle that said HENRY CAHILL 3 TIMES DAILY WITH MEALS MAY CAUSE DIZZINESS OR NAUSEA 5 REFILLS. The lenses were big and silver colored, like mirrors, which meant that no one could see him now—not really. In his opinion, this was a good thing. And they made the world look very blue to him. Blue trees, blue buildings, blue clouds, blue people.

Is the East Gate clear? The Secretary of State will be arriving in approximately two minutes. . . .

The old ladies were on the wide blue lawn, doing their early morning exercises. Nana had called it *tie cheese*. She was leading them, dressed in stretchy pants and a flowing cotton shirt. Angerman remembered that the Keeper women dressed that way, too. Nana's shirt billowed around her up and down, up and down as she moved her arms in the air in slow motion.

"Keep your knees bent, ladies," Nana called out. "Keep your hips loose. Miriam, come back, we're not done yet. Up—one, two, three. Down—one, two, three . . ."

In the distance, Angerman saw Hunter emerge from the main building with two large jugs of water. The boy put them in one of the golf carts, then rushed back inside, then emerged again with a duffel bag. Hunter had announced at breakfast that they, the older kids, would be leaving for Pisgah Island right after lunch. Hunter had said "older kids," then looked at Mommy, Teacher, and Cory. He had not looked at Angerman.

"Up—one, two, three. Down— What's the matter, Alice, is your bursitis bothering you?"

On the ground, a stream of small blue ants marched in formation around Angerman's right sneaker. Some of them bore tiny crumbs of food. What were the crumbs? Pieces of dead insects? Insects the ants had killed, just so they could eat a meal, for God's sake? Angerman felt rage swell in his chest. He lifted his right sneaker and brought it down on the ants and ground his heel back and forth.

"Young man, have you seen your father?"

Angerman glanced up. The grandma called Mrs. Johnson was staring at him with her milky blue eyes. She had wandered away from the others, who were twirling around in slow, dreamy circles on the blue lawn.

"I said, have you seen your father?"

Answer her, punk! It's not polite to keep the old fossil waiting, Bad Guy rasped.

Angerman felt the mannequin pulling on his hair, a tuft of it right next to his ear. Angerman winced.

You think that hurts? I'll show you what pain really *is.*

Mrs. Johnson blinked at Angerman. He opened his mouth and moved his lips.

"Yes, I know," Mrs. Johnson said. "But today's not a school day, is it? Will you tell him that I baked a banana cream pie for him?"

Angerman nodded. Mrs. Johnson took his hand. "Come on."

Angerman let her lead him over to the other grandmas. Her skin felt cool and brittle. He could probably snap her in two, this tiny old grandma with her wool cardigan and patched and stained flower-print dress and talcum-powdery hospital smell.

Mrs. Johnson and Angerman joined the grandmas in the front row. Nana glanced at them briefly and smiled and raised her arms in the air. Mrs. Johnson did the same, lifting her thin arms in a feeble wave.

"You have to do it, too," Mrs. Johnson whispered to Angerman. "It's good for the osteoporosis."

Angerman nodded. Then he raised his arms in the air, like Nana and Mrs. Johnson and the other grandmas were doing. His armpits stank. The straps of his backpack dug into his shoulders. Bad Guy pressed his cold plastic lips against his ear and said, *What, you one of the ladies now? You a girly-boy?*

Angerman jerked. His arms twitched in the air as he twirled around in slow motion.

Maybe you'll get your period soon, like Mommy.

Next to him, a grandma in a frayed nightgown began sobbing. Kirsten, who was on the other side of her, reached over and held her. Several of the grandmas stopped dancing and just stood there looking sad. The other grandmas continued with their dreamy movements.

Angerman continued with his movements, too. Something shiny caught his eye. Sunlight was glinting off the smashed windowpane of the main building. Through the jagged opening, Angerman saw Cory lifting Puppy in the air, then Kitty.

Blue, everything looked blue. The grandma's sobs

and the high-pitched squeals of the twins mingled with Bad Guy's horrible chattering—*if you find me you're gonna die, you're all gonna die, do you hear me, punk?* Angerman waved his arms and twirled, and thought about the dead ants. He wondered what death felt like. He wondered what it would feel like to kill someone, for real.

The noon sun blazed and made the air shimmer. In the driveway, Nana and the other grandmas gathered around the two golf carts. Hunter was sitting in one of them. Angerman was sitting next to him, shaking his head as if in a dispute but not saying anything.

Nearby, an egret swooped down and picked its way through an overgrown patch of grass. The goats grazed and *maaaed*. Nana whispered something to her mother, Mrs. Johnson, who was acting agitated.

Cory told herself to be brave as she hugged Puppy and Kitty one last time.

"I'll be back soon, okay?" she said in a high, cheerful voice. "We just have to go . . . go help a man, and then we'll be right back."

It was clear from the twins' expressions that they didn't even know what a "man" was. Or why Cory, Mommy, Teacher, Hunter, and Angerman were going on a trip without them.

Puppy barked. Kitty meowed. They wrapped their arms around Cory's neck and squeezed their bodies against hers. The smell of their skin made her heart hurt. She felt Kitty touch her short, bristly hair in the back.

"We'd better get going," Hunter said, glancing up at the sky. "I want to try to make it to Verona Beach before dark."

"Okay." Cory kissed Puppy's cheek, then Kitty's. "Be good, okay? Listen to Nana and Kirsten. Play with the baby goats."

Puppy and Kitty's heads bobbed up and down. Cory's eyes stung with tears. She turned abruptly to Teacher, who was loading a basket of carrots, radishes, and oranges in the back of the other golf cart. "Can I ride with you?" she said, swiping a hand across her nose.

"I'll ride with you guys, too," Mommy said quickly.

Hunter extracted a map from his back pocket and began unfolding it with a loud rustling noise.

"Sure," Teacher said to Cory and Mommy. "We can take turns driving."

Just then, Teddy Bear ran up to Teacher and burst into tears. Teacher bent down and hugged him and whispered something in his ear.

Cory glanced around, wondering where the other children were. She spotted Baby and Doll squeezed together on a white lawn chair, kicking their heels back into empty space.

"Dolly should have her physical today," Doll insisted.

"Nopey, uh-uh, Dolly should have her physical *yesterday*," Baby argued.

"But she feels bad *today*."

Cory didn't see Action Figure anywhere. The boy had rushed off in a sulk earlier because Hunter wouldn't let him go to Pisgah with them.

Nana walked up to Cory and Mommy. "Don't you worry about the little ones," she said in a quiet voice. "I'll take good care of them."

Mommy's mouth quivered. "I hate to leave them. But they'll be safer here than where we're going."

"That's right. You just go do what you have to do and get back here quick as you can, okay?" Nana said, patting Mommy's arm. "I know you feel you have to go look, but don't get your hopes up too high, okay?"

Mommy nodded. "'kay."

Teacher extracted herself from Teddy Bear and got behind the steering wheel. Cory climbed in next to her. Mommy climbed into the back.

"Okay, let's do it," Cory said.

Hunter and Teacher put their keys in the ignitions. The golf carts whirred to life. The last thing Cory saw as they lurched down the driveway was the sight of Teddy Bear, Baby, Doll, and the twins—Ingrid's beautiful baby twins—running after them, waving good-bye.

By the time they reached Verona Beach, it was almost dark. Mommy and Teacher collected wood for a campfire. Hunter and Cory spread the vegetables out on the seat of one of the carts.

Mommy was tired, so tired, but it wasn't from the long drive or the heat or even the bleeding. She was tired of listening to Angerman ranting. After being nearly silent for several days, he had started up again. He had ranted during the entire drive from the Woods to Verona Beach. His croaky voice had droned on and on over the whirring of the golf carts, the shrieking of seagulls, the shushing of waves.

Mommy sighed as she picked up another pine branch and added it to the growing collection in her arms. She breathed in the salty air and stared up at the deep blue sky between the boughs and needles of the wind-twisted pines. To the right, the surf washed onto the beach with almost silent wavelets. Ahead, the road stretched onward, hugging the coast and weaving in and out among trees.

She was tired, her stomach hurt, and she missed the little kids. It shocked her, even now, that she had agreed to leave them behind, even though she knew it was for the best. Still, she hoped that it was worth it, being separated from them in order to save President. If President needed saving. If President was even alive.

He had to be. There had to be a point to all of this.

"This just in!" Angerman shouted as he pounded a stick that had gotten jammed in the wheel of one of the carts. He whacked it with a rock. "The war between the government and the rebel forces has escalated to a new high. Today on Pisgah Island, Crackers the Clown entertained a group of five-year-olds during a birthday party for the New Savior, who declined the cupcakes. That sugary stuff can kill you! And speaking of which, Bad Guy, looks like *your* time is almost up!"

"Angerman, shut up," Hunter snapped, for what seemed like the hundredth time today.

He glanced over his shoulder at Teacher. Not at *her*, Mommy noticed. "That's probably enough wood for now. The matches are in the green duffel bag."

Before Teacher could say anything, Angerman extracted the Bad Guy mannequin from his backpack. "Did you hear me?" he screamed. "Your time is *up*! You're *dead*! We're gonna *get* you, Dad Guy!"

Hunter rose to his feet. "Angerman!"

Angerman brought his rock down on Bad Guy's face. He pounded and pounded, spit cascading from his mouth, his shoulders rising and heaving. Pieces of plastic flew through the air. Angerman's knuckles began bleeding.

Mommy dropped the firewood she was carrying and rushed up to Angerman. "Angerman, stop it! You're hurt!"

Angerman glanced down at the mannequin's face. Its right eye was completely bashed and dented in. Its face was smeared with Angerman's blood.

"Why won't you die?" Angerman said and began sobbing. "Why won't you just die?"

Mommy put her hand on Angerman's arm. But Angerman wrenched his arm away. Still sobbing, he reached into his backpack again. This time, he pulled out a small silver pistol. Mommy's stomach made a sickening lurch.

"That's Nana's gun!" Hunter cried out. "Angerman, give me that!"

"Angerman, where did you get that?" Cory demanded.

Angerman took the gun and pointed it at Bad Guy's head. "Why . . . won't . . . you . . . just . . . die?" he cried out.

"Angerman," Mommy whispered. "Please. Just give me the gun."

Her heart hammering in her chest, Mommy reached a trembling hand toward the gun. But Angerman pulled away from her. He stood up and flung Bad Guy's head toward the waves. It landed on a wet patch of sand and rolled around, startling a seagull that flew away with a loud flapping of wings.

Angerman collapsed to his knees and continued sobbing. He cradled the gun against his chest. He opened his mouth to speak, but nothing came out.

Mommy wrenched her gaze away from him, sick with pity and fear. Hunter was looking at her. He mouthed the words: "Tomorrow. We're going back."

Chapter Nine

Teacher awoke to the sound of a bird chattering kack-kack-kack somewhere very nearby. She tried to hang on to sleep, hunching her thin jacket up higher on her shoulder, but now that she was conscious she felt every bump and lump in the sand. The surf shushed from nearby, and she tried to let it lull her back to sleep. Then an insect crawled across her cheek and Teacher sat up with a jolt, swatting at her face.

"Uggh." She groaned.

She glanced at the sleeping forms around her—Mommy, Cory, Hunter—and her stomach rolled over. At the same instant she saw Angerman was missing, she noticed that one of the golf carts was missing, too. The noisy bird chattered *kack-kack-kack* again.

"Wake up, you guys!" Teacher said, scrambling to her feet. She stumbled as the sand shifted under her feet, but she lurched to Mommy and shook her arm. "Wake up! He's gone!"

"What?"

They each struggled awake and tried to snap from sleep to full alert in a heartbeat. Cory took a swig from a water bottle, and swished it around in her mouth before spitting it into the sand. "Do you think he heard us talking?" she speculated.

"No, no, no," Mommy said, shaking her head with a look of utter despair in her eyes. "What have we done?"

Hunter studied the tracks in the dust of the road. "He must've gone on ahead of us. Look how the tire marks keep going."

"But they didn't even have any power left when we stopped!" Teacher said, feeling an odd surge of anger. "That doesn't make any sense." She began leafing through The Book, the pages snapping and popping as she shoved them aside.

Mommy climbed up a low dune and looked toward the beach. "He took Bad Guy—the head isn't there anymore," she said, striding back down again.

Cory joined Hunter and walked on a few paces, her gaze on the ground. "He pushed it—see the footprints between the tire tracks? As soon as there's enough sunshine, it'll power up and he'll keep going. He wants to get to Pisgah Island first."

"Why?" Mommy wailed. "What is he going to—"

Everyone turned to look at Mommy as she broke off. Teacher felt a chill pass over her, and she knew they were all thinking the same thing. "Where's the gun?" she whispered.

"Wait a minute, wait a minute!" Hunter said, holding up his hands and backing off. "He wouldn't do anything crazy. . . ." His voice trailed off.

"Sure he would. He *is* crazy," Cory said in a matter-of-fact tone.

"But who would he want to hurt?" Mommy said. "If he thinks President is there, maybe he wants to rescue him? Kill Supreme Leader to save President?"

Teacher let her breath out very slowly and began searching near the beginning of The Book for a particular page. "'Killing Is Wrong: Vote for Death Penalty Reform!'"

"What?" Cory asked, rubbing her bristly scalp.

"There's a thing called Ten Commandments," Teacher explained. "I remembered it from the Before Time. They're rules. Important rules, like dos and don'ts. I didn't know what order they go in, but I finally got all ten."

She held up The Book so Cory could read the pasted-in clippings.

Don't Delay! Accept No Substitutes!
Say No to Drugs!
Call for a Free Estimate!
Don't Let a Little Rain Spoil Your Day! ***Just Do It!***
Stop Throwing Money Down the Drain!
Killing Is Wrong: Vote for Death Penalty Reform!
Keep America Beautiful! **Have It Your Way!**

"Are you sure these are commandments?" Cory asked as she struggled through the words. "We had different ones back at the Crossroads. How do you even know these are rules?"

"That line and dot thing is called examination point," Teacher said. "It goes on rules, and I guess people used to give examinations about them. That makes sense, right, that they'd give examinations about something as important as the Ten Commandments?"

Cory was puzzling out the words one at a time. "Don't ask me," she said. "We had a lot more than ten rules at the Crossroads, but I don't think any of their rules were the real ones from before. What does that one mean, *Just Do It*? Do what?"

"Well, I guess it means if you decide to do something

you should go ahead and do it," Teacher said with a shrug. "Some are easy to understand, like the one about money. We used to play with money at first, but we sure never put it down the drain. And the one about killing—that's pretty clear."

"And so's the first one," Mommy said. "'Don't Delay.' Let's get going and catch Angerman before he does something bad."

Pushing the golf cart was easy with four people—one to steer and three to push. Mommy couldn't help believing that they'd catch up to Angerman, even with his head start. But as the morning wore on and the sun began charging the solar cells, it was obvious that Angerman would beat them. The speed of the cart with four of them in it was so slow it would almost be faster to walk.

"I bet his cart is going really fast, too," Cory muttered. She was actually striding alongside, having no trouble keeping up on foot.

"We'll catch him," Mommy said.

Ahead, the road climbed a gradual rise, and a stand of misshapen pine trees cast a long pool of shadow across the path. The cart whined as it strained to climb the incline, and then began stuttering and jerking through the shade. Mommy fought back the desire to scream. "C'mon, c'mon," she whispered, leaning forward.

"Just let it get out into the sunlight again," Hunter said. He jumped out, and put his shoulder to the back of the cart.

"This is crazy!" Teacher burst out. "What's the point of having a cart if nobody's riding in it?"

Cory helped Hunter push. "Least we don't have to

carry the food and water."

"No, we're not carrying it, we're pushing it," Hunter said under his breath.

Mommy stepped out of the cart, leaving Teacher at the steering wheel. With a short, abrupt jolt, the cart pulled forward out of the shadows into the full sunlight again. Teacher switched off the motor and sat fuming, her arms crossed over her chest.

"This time let's wait long enough for the cart to get a full amount of power," Teacher said with her jaw clenched. "It's no good just waiting long enough for it to start."

"Let's look at the map, see how much farther we have to go," Hunter suggested.

He wiped his forehead with one wrist: Mommy saw that his hair was stuck together into damp spikes at the back of his neck. When he turned his head she quickly looked away, so that he wouldn't catch her looking at him. While Teacher and Cory and Hunter examined the map, Mommy walked a few paces back into the shade where it was cooler.

Angerman's disappearance had rattled her much more than she had let on to the others. He had said something strange last night while she was trying to get the gun away from him, but she couldn't remember what it was. She had been so busy trying to calm him down, get him to stop acting so—so—so insane, that she couldn't put her finger on what exactly it was that had struck her as stranger than usual. The thought of him going on ahead, all alone, frightened and confused, with no one to help him, made her feel as though she was turning inside out.

Sometimes she wished he had never come to them in the first place. If it weren't for Angerman, they'd still be safely in Lazarus, living the life they had come to think of as normal. Ever since he'd come into their lives, they'd been in almost constant danger, fear, and confusion.

But they had been on the verge of starving before he came along, hiding in their familiar house and ignoring the truth that looked them in the eyes every day. Angerman had given them a purpose, given them something to look ahead to, gotten them moving. He was a terrifying spark of fire, their inspiration. He was their leader.

She picked up a fallen pine branch and flung it as hard as she could against the nearest tree. It hit with a loud crack, and a pair of squirrels ran chattering and squeaking through the boughs.

"This just in," she whispered. "We need you, Angerman."

The sun was well behind them to the west before they saw the first sign for Pisgah Island causeway. Hunter's heart gave a wild thump of excitement.

"We're getting close," he said, trying to keep his voice steady.

"Let's just hope this cart keeps going a while longer," Cory said.

She was gripping the steering wheel with white knuckles. Hunter wondered, with a flash of surprise, if she was scared. It was hard to imagine Cory being scared, but now it occurred to him that she had become very quiet as they drew closer to their destination—to the island where the Keepers were.

Tall grasses at the side of the road cast long, needle-thin shadows, and a meandering breeze bent the tops of the weeds here and there. Fortunately, the road had gone through bright, unshadowed sun since their quick lunch break, and the cart had gone steadily—if not at lightning speed. A little bit more was all the machine had to deliver. Once within range, Hunter knew they would be better off on foot, anyway.

"There's his track," Mommy spoke up. She pointed to the tire marks of Angerman's cart ahead of them.

Hunter glanced at her. She had pointed out Angerman's track every time it had been visible, as though she thought he'd be right around the next bend. With a frown, Hunter tipped the map toward the failing light. As far as he could tell, they had to cross a creek, and then the road to the island would bear off to the right.

"Bridge ahead," Teacher spoke up.

"This is it!" Hunter gasped. He crushed the map down between the seats and leaned out of the cart to survey the road.

Cory slowed the cart as they neared the bridge, and they saw a faded and rust-streaked sign bolted to the cement pylon on the left: OCA CREEK. The bridge itself was intact. The cart purred over, and Hunter had a glimpse of flat, slow-moving water below, and toward the right a salty marsh stretched toward the wide sky. The ocean was over there, but out of earshot and obscured by tall grasses and swamp trees.

"Pretty soon there's gonna be a road on the right," he said.

The four kids were silent as they drove onward.

From the top of a dead tree in the marsh, an eagle swooped downward to pluck a fish from the water and carried it off. The road curved around an old gas station whose roof had caved in, and then there was another road heading straight toward the ocean.

Cory stepped on the brake. "Is this it?"

"There's no sign," Teacher pointed out.

Hunter jumped out; he examined the road that continued parallel to the coast and this new one, making for the water. The road continuing onward was drifted with sand, and there was no evidence of any traffic going that way, whereas the road to the right showed signs of a lot of use. Hunter pictured the Keepers' chariots coming this way, and then with a cry of discovery he spotted a pile of dried-out horse droppings.

"This is it," he exulted. "This has to be the way."

Nodding, Cory shifted the gear lever to forward, but the cart lurched once and the motor cut off. The wheels carried it forward for a foot or so until it rolled to a stop.

"Okay," Mommy said, climbing out. "So we walk the rest of the way."

Teacher stood rubbing her chin and eyeing the road to the island. "Let's get this cart a little bit hidden," she suggested. "That way it'll charge up in the morning, and as long as no one finds it, we can get out of here."

"Good idea."

Hunter put his shoulder to the cart while Cory steered. Once they had it out of sight around a bend of the unused part of the main road, they grabbed their food and water. The road out to the island was sandy and soft underfoot, but the grassy ridge between the wheel tracks made for firmer walking. They went single file, their shadows stretching straight out ahead of them. The marsh spread out on either side of the causeway, and tall stilt-legged birds hunted for fish and frogs in the reeds. A blackbird perched on a swaying stem and voiced loud and shrill into the twilight.

Hunter felt as if all the nerves and muscles in his body were quivering and tingling. Now that they might actually be nearing their goal—of finding the president—he was alive with excitement. If the president was really there, really a prisoner of the Keepers, and they *rescued* him—they would be like the superheroes he remembered from car tunes. He knew it was dangerous, but he couldn't help smiling, and he was glad they were walking single file so the others wouldn't see the big grin on his face.

The road began to climb a rise: Hunter could see that it was a man-made hill, and that it led to a bridge going over another meandering creek. A large signpost at the side of the road said PRIVATE: NO TRESPASSING. Hunter raised a hand to signal the girls behind him.

"The island is ahead," he warned. "Let's go slow now and no talking."

"We aren't talking," Teacher grumbled.

He gave her a stern look, and then they crested the rise of the bridge. Beyond, the road swept down and across a narrow spit of land with ocean on either side and joined to a wooded island. Even from here Hunter could tell the place had once been well-protected: a guardhouse and gate barred the end of the road. Hunter lay down on his belly, waiting for the others to do the same.

"There's somebody standing at that gate," Teacher said.

Hunter squinted. The glasses he had found at the Crossroads were good but not good enough for him to see a person that far away. "You're sure?"

"Yes. I see him, too," Cory muttered. "A Keeper."

They watched silently for a few moments, while the air grew cool against their backs. Mommy picked up a bleached shell and turned it over in her fingers, frowning in concentration.

"What are they guarding against?" she asked at last.

Hunter turned to look at her. "What do you mean?"

"Why do they need a guard? There's nobody left," Mommy explained.

"Maybe they know we're coming," Teacher whispered. "Maybe they caught Angerman, and . . . and maybe they know we're coming," she repeated weakly.

An odd ripple of pleasure made Hunter smile. He was delighted to think the Keepers felt they needed to post a guard against them—it meant they were a force to be reckoned with.

"We'll have to wait for dark," Hunter said, masking his excitement. He was sure Mommy wouldn't approve of how he was feeling. "Then we'll sneak in."

"There's another reason maybe for the guard," Cory spoke up.

They all looked at her, waiting.

"Maybe there *are* some others left," she said.

For a moment, nobody spoke. The idea was almost frightening. Frightening, because it could lead to hope.

"We're here because we think the president could have survived," Cory said. "So why couldn't some others have survived, too? Just because we haven't met any others doesn't mean they aren't out there."

Mommy clenched the shell in her fist. "Maybe," she whispered, her eyes aglow. "Maybe there are."

Teacher reached into her knapsack and pulled The Book out. "Okay, before it gets totally dark, take a look at this," she said, pulling out a picture. "This is who we're looking for. The president."

Hunter studied the picture. The man almost looked familiar. "I think I remember him," he said in an uncertain voice, "from the Before Time."

"I think I do, too," Mommy added.

Cory tugged her soldier's hat down a little lower on her forehead. "Okay, then. Soon as it gets dark, we'll go see what we can see."

Chapter Ten

A cold, salty breeze blew against Teacher's face as she sat by the side of the road, poring over The Book. The sky was purple with twilight, and thick black clouds kept passing over the moon. Hunter wouldn't let her use a flashlight, in case the Keeper at the guardhouse might see, which meant that she was forced to interpret The Book's holy messages in bits and pieces—whenever the moon wasn't hiding behind a cloud.

She *had* to get some answers, though. Her family was about to undertake its most dangerous mission yet: sneaking into the Keepers' den and maybe rescuing the president of the United States of America. And maybe Angerman, too, if he was crazy enough to have done what they all guessed he had done, which was to go in there alone with nothing but Nana's gun and that creepy mannequin head. In Teacher's opinion, Angerman was crazy enough to do just that—and more.

"Is it dark enough yet, do you think?" Cory spoke up. She was sitting on the other side of the road, scraping the blade of her jackknife against her boot. Hunter was sitting next to her, sipping from a water bottle. Mommy was next to Teacher, arranging and rearranging a pile of pebbles.

"Yes," Hunter said.

"No!" Mommy said at the exact same moment.

Hunter and Mommy stared at each other. Hunter

swiped the back of his hand across his mouth.

"Well, which is it?" Cory said. "We can't wait forever. If Angerman's in there . . . well, he might do something stupid." She snapped her blade shut.

"I think we should wait a little while until it's really, really pitch-black," Mommy insisted. "That guard is still there. We can't take any chances."

"I don't know," Cory murmured.

Teacher still wasn't used to the way Cory looked—like a boy with her soldier's uniform and her new short, fuzzy haircut, but like a girl in every other way. Teacher thought about Nana's talk, about periods. Cory made periods. Now, Mommy made periods, too. She, Teacher, was the only one who didn't make periods, except for the little ones.

Teacher picked up her pen. She wanted to scrawl that word *period* in The Book. But maybe it wasn't important enough. Maybe that word was more about her own frustration at being different from Mommy and Cory. Teacher put the pen down and sighed. She had to keep searching for answers that would be relevant to the whole family, to their mission at hand. Time was running out, and this wasn't about her.

Scowling, Hunter took another swig from his water bottle. "I'm with Cory. We can't wait too much longer. Just a few minutes, okay?"

Mommy moved a pebble from the top of the pile to the bottom. "'kay."

Teacher turned the pages of The Book. The pictures that had come loose at the corners flapped and fluttered in the breeze. There had to be something . . . *anything*. Was the family right to try to sneak onto Pisgah Island?

Was President still alive? Was Angerman there? Was *he* still alive? What was the best way to stay hidden from the Keepers, who would surely want to take the four of them prisoner—or worse?

Teacher got to the page with the Ten Commandments. It occurred to her that maybe, just maybe, these holy rules could guide them in their mission.

She touched the first rule with her fingertips. *Don't Delay!* That must mean they should go in there now, like Hunter and Cory were saying. Her fingertips trailed across the page. *Accept No Substitutes!* She remembered a thing called substitute teacher, from the Before Time. That rule must mean that she, Teacher, was to be part of this mission and not someone *pretending* to be her. *Say No to Drugs!* Maybe the Keepers would try to hurt them with drugs, and they had to say no? *Call for a Free Estimate!* Teacher didn't know what an estimate was, but the word *free* made sense, since that's what they were here to do—free President and Angerman. *Don't Let a Little Rain Spoil Your Day!* That must mean that even if it started raining, they shouldn't give up. *Just Do It!* Yes, they should just do it—but when and how? *Stop Throwing Money Down the Drain!* That one still confused her. And what did it have to do with the Keepers, if anything? *Killing Is Wrong: Vote for Death Penalty Reform!* That meant the Keepers shouldn't kill them, and they shouldn't kill the Keepers, either, especially not with Nana's gun, which could make a lot of blood. *Keep America Beautiful!* Well, that probably used to be President's job, and if they rescued him, he could go back to doing it again. *Have It Your Way!* That sounded cheerful and optimistic, like maybe the family was going to succeed and win—and the Keepers were going to lose.

Teacher sighed and turned a couple more pages. She stopped. There was something on page 124 that she had never noticed before.

Goose bumps prickled her arms. "Oh, *no*."

Mommy leaned over. "What is it, Teacher? What does The Book say?"

Teacher pointed to page 124. Across a newspaper picture of a man in a dark robe—FATHER FLANAGAN GREETS THE RESIDENTS OF SEASIDE ON EASTER MORNING!—were a bunch of words scribbled in red ink:

DIE
DIE
DIE
DIE
DIE

Mommy clasped a hand over her mouth. "Why would The Book tell us *that*?" she whispered. "I thought you said The Book said killing was *wrong*."

"I don't think The Book is telling us this," Teacher said, barely able to conceal her rage. "Don't you see? *Angerman* wrote in The Book. He did this!"

"What's going on?"

Cory crawled over to Mommy and Teacher on her hands and knees and peered at The Book. "Wow," she said after a moment. "But when would he have done this? You always keep The Book with you," she pointed out to Teacher.

"I don't know. Maybe he did it last night, while we were all sleeping." With a trembling hand, Teacher touched the words Angerman had written. The point of his pen had gouged deep grooves into the paper. There was even a rip where one of the *I*s should have been.

"Look, the guard's gone," Hunter said suddenly.

The three girls glanced up. Hunter was on his feet, adjusting his glasses. "That guard just went inside," he said in a low, excited voice. "Come on, this is our chance."

"But what if he comes right back?" Mommy said, wiping her hands on her skirt.

"That's why we have to move *now*," Hunter replied. "Come *on*!"

Teacher could tell Mommy wasn't happy about this. Neither was she, especially not after what she had just discovered in The Book. She had not found the answers she had been searching for—just more confusion and Angerman's craziness.

Still, Hunter—and Cory—were right. The four of them couldn't waste any more time, especially if President and Angerman were on the island. And now was their opportunity, with the Keeper having abandoned his post for the moment. *Don't Delay!*

A cloud passed over the moon. Teacher closed The Book, tucked it under her arm, and got to her feet. She followed Hunter and Cory down the dirt road. Mommy trailed behind her, breathing hard.

The gentle sounds of the waves mingled with the chirping of crickets and the occasional distant cry of some wild animal. Without the moon, it was so dark that

Teacher had a hard time seeing her own feet in front of her.

Then a second later the moon appeared again, and the night landscape was bathed in a cool silver glow. Hunter walked up to the gate and peered in. "Just a driveway and a whole lotta trees," he whispered. "Come on, this way."

To the right and the left of the gate and guardhouse was a wrought-iron fence that seemed to go on and on. Hunter went off to the left, hugging the fence. Teacher, Cory, and Mommy followed him. Through the iron fence, through the thick woods just beyond it, Teacher thought she could make out a glowing point of light. It flickered in and out of sight between trunks and leaves.

"This place seems deserted," Cory observed. "Besides that guard, there's nobody—*ow*!"

"What happened?" Teacher demanded.

"I kicked a rock or something," Cory grumbled. She bent down. "No, not a rock—*this*. Guys, he *is* here!"

"Who's here?" Hunter asked her.

In reply, Cory held up Bad Guy's head. Illuminated by moonlight, it looked especially horrible. One eye was totally gouged out. Its blood-streaked face was badly scratched up and dented from all of Angerman's beatings.

"He *is* here." Mommy gasped. "But why would he leave Dad Guy—I mean, Bad Guy—behind?"

"Who knows why Angerman does anything?" Hunter said with a shrug. "C'mon, we've gotta keep going. Look, I think I see an opening in the fence. That'll be safer than going in through the front gate."

Cory tucked the mannequin head under her arm and

marched after Hunter. Teacher thought she looked like a bizarre war god from the Geek mists. Hunter stopped in front of a place in the fence where some bars were missing. He bent down and squeezed through the hole. Cory did the same, and then Teacher, and then finally, Mommy.

Teacher yanked a burr out of her sleeve and glanced around. There was nothing but woods as far as she could see. She could still make out the point of light in the distance. She wondered if it was coming from a house. Nana had said President and his family used to vacation at Pisgah Island, which meant that there had to be a house.

Except now, it wasn't President's house anymore but the Keepers' house.

Teacher shuddered and turned to Hunter. "Now what?"

"Now you're coming with us."

The kids whirled around. Two men stepped out from behind a couple of large pine trees. They were carrying spears in their hands. The razor-sharp points gleamed in the moonlight.

Hunter, Cory, and Mommy froze. Teacher clasped The Book to her chest and hugged it tightly. Closing her eyes, she began going through its prayer words in her head—*cyberspace, Chevrolet, strawberry preserves made from 100% strawberries*—but nothing helped, none of them comforted her.

Teacher opened her eyes and stared at the shiny tips of the spears. The Keepers obviously didn't think that killing was wrong. The Keepers were going to kill them, she was sure of it. They had probably already killed President and Angerman, too.

"You must be the kids who tried to burn down the Crossroads," one of the guards said.

"No, we're not!" Mommy lied. Cory sucked in a deep breath.

"Supreme Leader has been expecting you all," the other guard added. "He's in the middle of a ceremony right now. But as soon as he's finished, he's going to want to welcome you in person."

"What does that mean?" Hunter demanded.

The first guard smiled. "You'll see."

The Keeper guards marched them through the dark woods, their heavy footsteps crushing twigs and brush. Nobody spoke. Cory could tell that Hunter wanted to do *something*—attack the guards from behind, maybe—because he kept turning around and making funny signals to her with his hands. But they both knew it was useless to act, at least for the moment. The guards had weapons, and the four of them had nothing. Cory held the mannequin head higher under her arm, pushed back her shoulders, and tried very hard not to show her fear.

Cory hadn't recognized the guards, and they apparently hadn't recognized her. Not as Corinthians 1:19, anyway. Perhaps there were Keepers who lived on Pisgah Island and never came to the Crossroads? But she knew that Deuteronomy 29:28 and other Keepers went back and forth between the two places. She also knew that *she* had originally been destined to come to Pisgah, to be a Handmaid. Whatever that was. She suspected that other young girls had come to Pisgah before her, to be Handmaids, too. Would she see any of the ones she knew from the Crossroads, like Colossians 3:18 or

Hosea 2:19? They had disappeared so quickly and mysteriously.

Soon, a house became visible through the trees. It was an enormous house, with big windows and shutters and a wraparound porch with lots of rocking chairs. The empty chairs teetered back and forth in the wind. Beyond the house, Cory could make out a black sliver of ocean and beach.

"This way," one of the guards said, pointing to a path with his spear. "Supreme Leader is over in the meeting hall."

"Is there . . . did a boy come here?" Mommy spoke up.

The guards looked at her and laughed.

"This way. No questions!"

The guards made the four of them go down the path before them. Cory felt something sharp poking into her back. She realized that one of the guards was touching her with his spear, and she had to resist the temptation to turn around and grab the spear from him. She wasn't a weak, obedient little Keeper girl anymore. The jerk! She tightened her grip on Bad Guy and hurried her steps.

The meeting hall was a big barn on the other side of the house. Two small square windows flickered with firelight. Cory could just make out the low drone of a male voice coming from inside and a chorus of other voices chanting, "By the Flame!"

Her heart thumped in her chest. She was about to come face-to-face with Supreme Leader. And Supreme Leader knew everything, or so she had been told. Which meant that he would be able to see through her boy disguise and know that she was Cory, Corinthians 1:19, the sinner, the heathen, the fallen one—even if no one else in the place recognized her.

"Come on."

The guards led them to a wide door and opened it. Cory took a deep breath and stepped inside.

The meeting hall was filled with dozens of Keeper men and women. They were dressed in the traditional Keeper costumes—blue for the men, white for the women—and holding torches high in the air. They were facing forward and watching something, listening to someone.

"The bride is to the man as man is to God," a male voice droned.

"By the Flame!"

"By the Flame!"

The flames from the torches licked the air and made grotesque shadows on the walls. Cory, Mommy, Teacher, and Hunter scrunched against the door, flanked on either side by the two guards. Cory felt Mommy's hand creep into hers, and she squeezed it tight.

"The bride shall bear the child of the man, and the child shall be a servant of God."

"By the Flame!"

Puppy and Kitty. Cory saw their faces in her mind. She wondered what they were doing now, back at the Woods. She wondered if they missed her. She wondered if they were afraid.

As people shifted to make way for her, Cory suddenly had a view of the front of the room. She saw that an elderly preacher was conducting a ceremony. In front of him was a dark-haired man. Cory couldn't see his face because he had his back turned to the crowd. Next to the man was a woman in a wedding dress. A long white wedding dress, like the one Cory had on when she'd run away from the Crossroads.

Then the woman turned her face slightly, and Cory realized with a start that she wasn't a woman at all. She was Ephesians 5:6 from the Crossroads. And she was fourteen, just like Cory.

Ice water coursed through Cory's veins. The dark-haired man had to be Supreme Leader. She had only seen him once in person, and now his back was to her, but she was sure of it. That was Supreme Leader, and Effie was being married to him.

That's what it meant to be a Handmaid. It meant getting married to Supreme Leader, being his wife.

"The bride shall serve her husband and her God all the rest of her days. . . ."

Cory felt Mommy's nails dig into her hand. Cory yanked her hand away, almost dropping Bad Guy's head as she did so. *"What?"*

Mommy pointed with a trembling finger. "It's him. It's *Angerman*," she whispered.

"Where?"

Then Cory saw. Angerman was standing to the left of Supreme Leader. He was wearing a blue shirt and pants, just like the other Keeper men. His long, tangly brown hair had been smoothed back into a neat ponytail.

"What's going on?" Hunter hissed. "What's *he* doing up there dressed that way?"

The room erupted into shouting and clapping, and the man and the bride and Angerman all turned around. People raised their torches in the air and rushed up to congratulate the newly married couple.

Supreme Leader waved his hand and smiled a wide,

benevolent smile. His eyes scanned the room and fell on Cory and then moved on.

Cory felt as though she had stopped breathing.

The dark-haired man definitely was Supreme Leader.

But Supreme Leader was also President J. Colin McDowell.

Chapter Eleven

Mommy couldn't make her brain work. Her head was spinning. Here was Supreme Leader. Here was the president. Same man. She couldn't make that make sense, even though she could see with her own eyes it was true. Teacher was staring at the photograph and looking up at the smiling groom, then back to the picture and back again to the man. Around them, Keepers were shaking hands and giving the kiss of peace, and giving their warmest wishes to the bride—who looked more terrified than delighted. Angerman was shaking hands with people, too, and grinning from ear to ear as though he was the father of the bride and glad to be rid of her. He was one of them, a Keeper of the Flame. He was one of the enemy.

"But—but—" Hunter stammered.

"Hi, you guys," Angerman said in a casual way, sauntering over to join them.

For a moment, they could only stare at him, speechless. Then Mommy burst out, "What's going on? I don't get it! Have you been lying to us all along?"

"Yeah, isn't he the president?" Teacher added. "He's really the head of all the Keepers?"

Angerman looked back over his shoulder, and the flickering torchlight threw his face into deep shadow. Then he looked back again. All traces of his former talking problem were gone. "Well, sure. How else could they pull off such a huge plan?"

Again, they stared at him uncomprehending. Angerman smiled, as if they were kidding him. "*You* know," he said, giving Cory a playful punch in the arm.

"No, we don't know," Cory growled.

He sighed with impatience. "*Fire-us.*"

A wave of cold spread through Mommy's bloodstream. "*What?*"

"Oh, come *on*, Mommy," Angerman said. Two men standing nearby glanced over at Angerman's raised voice. "How else could we cleanse the world? It had to be cleansed with fire—to make way for the Second Coming."

Cory was trembling—whether with fear or with rage, Mommy couldn't be sure. The girl's face was white, but two red splotches glowed high on her cheekbones. "The Great Flame."

"Bingo," Angerman crowed. He lowered his gaze for a moment to the scarred and bloodstained head tucked under Cory's arm, and his smile wavered. For a second he seemed to choke, but then he tore his glance away. He made an obvious effort to smile. "Clean it all up and start over. That way, we knew that anyone born in the Year One or after could be the New Savior."

"By the Flame," a woman mumbled nearby. She looked over and smiled, and then went back to her conversation.

"By the Flame," Angerman repeated. "I hope you guys understand, this is how it had to be. The mission now is to find any kids born that year or since and test them."

Mommy was shaking her head, almost numb with disbelief. He was talking about Puppy and Kitty. From the very start, he had been especially interested in them, wanting to know how old they were, where they'd come from. He had been determined to take Puppy and Kitty with him to find the president—and all this time . . . "No. I don't believe you," she said aloud.

"Do you actually know what the Testing is?" Teacher demanded.

"It's called Trial by Fire," Angerman said in a casual tone. "I mean, I haven't actually *seen* it done yet, so I'm not exactly—"

"You were going to hand them to—"

Cory lunged toward him, but Hunter and Teacher grabbed her arms. Bad Guy's head clunked to the floor, and Mommy stooped to pick it up without thinking. She held the battered head gingerly, as though it might snap at her.

"Listen, listen," Angerman said, raising his voice enough so that some of the other Keepers nearby glanced their way again. "I know what you're thinking. You're thinking wow, all this time maybe Puppy or Kitty was the New Savior, but since they both died when we crossed that flooded river four days ago, neither one of them could have been the one. Otherwise they woulda survived."

Hunter gaped at him. "But—"

Teacher touched Hunter on the elbow to quiet him. "At least they didn't have to go through the Testing."

Slowly, uncertainly, Mommy nodded her head, her eyes locked on Angerman's. "Right," she said.

He held her gaze for a long moment. From the corner of her eye, Mommy noticed two of the men move with deliberate speed through the crowd toward a door. Then

Angerman gave them all a mock salute.

"Well, see you around."

Then he turned on his heel and melted into the crowd, stopping to shake hands and chitchat with the Keepers along the way.

Hunter could feel his heart pounding *thump-thump-thump* in his chest, and his breathing sounded harsh and loud to his own ears. These people, they had destroyed the world on purpose. They had released the Fire-us that killed all the First Mommies and First Daddies—his own parents, *everyone*—and to think he had wanted to be one of them when he first arrived at the Crossroads. Hunter was horrified to discover he was on the brink of tears. And now Angerman was—what was he, sane? Crazy? One of them or one of the Keepers? Hunter squeezed his eyes shut, wishing he could blot it all out.

"What's he doing?" Teacher hissed as Angerman walked away. "Is he or isn't he one of them?"

"Yeah, what's that stuff about Puppy and Kitty?" Cory said, her expression fierce.

"Just go along," Mommy whispered. She jerked her head to the right. "Shh."

Hunter turned to see Supreme Leader—President—walking toward them with his young bride. The girl looked no older than Mommy or Cory, and Hunter felt himself blushing. That man was now that girl's husband. That didn't seem right at all. Hunter blushed even deeper.

"Well, you must be the kids who stayed with our Brothers and Sisters at the Crossroads," the president said. He appraised them, a trace of a smile on his face as he looked them up and down. "And left in such a hurry, too."

"We're sorry about that fire," Hunter muttered. "It was an accident."

"Of course, of course," the president said. His smile widened, and he patted Hunter on the shoulder. His voice was warm and rich, and he seemed to be surrounded by an aura of strength, wisdom, and compassion. "We don't blame you."

For a moment, Hunter felt a surge of pride that he had been singled out by such a powerful man. Then his thoughts caught up with his emotions, and he backed away, frowning. He almost stepped on Cory's foot: she was standing directly behind him, trying to hide from Supreme Leader's sight.

President turned to Mommy, and his smile changed in some subtle way. Hunter didn't at all like the way the man was looking at Mommy. "I understand you had some very little children with you," the president said.

"They died!" Hunter spoke up, trying to deflect attention from Mommy. President looked at Hunter, the boy saw with relief. "There was an accident. And, so—so they're dead."

"That's right," Teacher added while the bride winced and sent a frightened look back over her shoulder as if she were searching for an escape route.

The president looked from one to the other of them, and his face was filled with sadness. "What a shame. That must have been very painful for you to see."

"Yeah," Hunter said.

"Well, I hope you'll be staying with us for a few days," the president went on. "You'll find we don't have any locks here, but I'm sure you won't want to leave us too soon."

Mommy shot Hunter a glance: they were prisoners, even if the president didn't say it in so many words. At once, Hunter understood the guards at the guardhouse: they kept people in, not out.

"And now if you'll excuse me," President McDowell continued, tucking his new bride's hand into the crook of his arm. "It is my wedding night."

With another dazzling smile, he turned and left them, leading the girl away. Men began taking down the torches from the wall, and the room grew darker and darker as the crowd left the building. Hunter, Teacher, Mommy, and Cory stood silent in the shadows, as if turned to stone.

I got away from them as soon as I could, I had to warn you, by the Flame . . . come on down, the prices have never been so low . . . trying to join you for months, but they stopped me . . . only doing my sacred duty . . . a fender bender on I-95 . . . don't trust them . . .

One of the Keeper men escorted Mommy, Teacher, Hunter, and Cory to a small cottage. Withered palm fronds littered the steps, and the front door was swollen with dampness. The man put his shoulder to the door and shoved, then jerked his chin toward the dark interior. A faint musty smell seeped out.

"You'll sleep here," he said.

Cory took a quick step to the side as he passed, keeping her face hidden by her hat brim. So far, she hadn't seen more than a couple of people she recognized, and she was pretty sure they hadn't seen her—which was a good thing, because a frightening plan was beginning to take shape inside her head. She followed Mommy and Teacher and Hunter inside, and as soon as she pushed the complaining door shut, the other three burst out talking at once, their voices bouncing around in the darkness.

"Isn't he creepy?"

"Do you think Angerman is planning to kill him?"

"Maybe he was planning it all along!"

Cory felt her way along the wall, her thoughts and emotions quarreling like two gulls jabbing and pecking at a dead crab. That man, Supreme Leader, President, whatever people called him, it was all *his* fault. He had unleashed a deadly disease that killed so many people—nearly everyone in the world—and he would kill Puppy and Kitty, too, if he had the chance. She had no illusion that any child would—or could—pass the Testing.

Her hands came upon a cold, spindly thing, and her mind said, *lamp*, before she continued on. Not even the dimmest ray of light came through the windows—if there were windows. Cory tried to see things from the corner of her eye, knowing that in such inky darkness, it was sometimes easier to see faint objects that way. But she could see nothing—nothing except Supreme Leader's smiling face. Rage surged up through her chest and throat, leaving a burning taste in her mouth. She wanted to pick up the lamp and smash it into that face, the way Angerman was always smashing Bad Guy's plastic head.

The others were still talking and feeling their way around the darkness of the cottage. There was a muffled grunt from Hunter as he banged into something.

"Sofa," he said.

"I found an easy chair," came Mommy's voice from

across the room. "Listen, if Angerman is planning to kill the president, that makes him the same as them. A killer."

"We don't even know if he still has that gun," Teacher said, moving away. "We need to find out if he has it, and if he does, get it away from him."

"Yeah, and then get out of here," Mommy added. "Now we know we're not getting any help from the president. The last person in the world we'll ever get help from."

Cory's shins bumped against something hard that started moving. *Rocking chair.* She felt for the back of the chair with hands that shook, then lowered herself into it. For a moment, she bent her head and crossed her arms over her knees, trying to calm the sensation of bitter anger that was making her shiver in spite of the heat.

"Do you think Angerman knew?" Teacher asked, her voice coming closer again. "Do you think he knew President did it? Nana said that when something terrible happens it can make you sick in your brain. If he knew President made Fire-us, maybe that's what made him so angry."

Nobody spoke for several seconds. Cory tried to stop shaking, but violent tremors kept blundering through her.

Angry. *Angry?* Now Cory knew why Angerman was crazy, because she thought she was in danger of going crazy, too. It was like having a stranger inside her body, this anger, this rage, this hatred. It was like some giant shadow thing that swelled and surged inside her blood. *Angry?*

"We've gotta get that gun," Hunter said, breaking the silence.

Cory nodded, even though she knew none of them could see her. As much as any of them, she wanted to get the gun away from Angerman. In fact, she wanted it more.

Because she was going to kill Supreme Leader—the president—herself.

Chapter Twelve

Mommy speared a piece of mango with her fork and brought it up to her lips. The mango slices were arranged on her plate in a fan shape next to a sun-dried tomato omelet and flat pieces of something called smoked salmon. She wasn't eating it, though. Smoking was what you did with drugs, and she knew the rule—*Say No to Drugs.* And anyway, it was oily looking and smelled like fish.

Supreme Leader—President—had asked them to join him for breakfast, and now they all were sitting at a table overlooking the beach: him, Mommy, Teacher, Hunter, and Cory. Mommy had no idea where Angerman was. Down below, waves rolled in and out, leaving broken shells, tendrils of seaweed, and strange-looking dead things on the damp sand.

Behind President, two guards in blue jeans and blue shirts stood still as statues. There were no other Keepers around, except for a woman who kept bringing them baskets of hot, buttered toast covered with white cloth napkins. The sun was bright—too bright—and Mommy had to shield her eyes with her hand as she listened to President speaking in his deep voice. It jarred her, his voice. It brought back memories of her First Daddy, reading newspaper headlines to her at the breakfast table.

"In the Millennium Year, the year God made me president of the United States so I could do His bidding, we all assumed that the Apocalypse would come," President McDowell said as he raised his coffee cup to his lips.

Under the table, Mommy could see that Teacher's fingers were twitching and trembling. She knew that her friend was dying for paper and a pen so she could write down everything President was saying, but The Book was hidden in a safe place—safe from the book-burning Keepers. Cory, her soldier's cap low over her forehead, was working intently on her food, as if she hadn't eaten in months. Hunter, on the other hand, had hardly touched his breakfast. Mommy saw that his eyes were bloodshot. It occurred to her that he probably hadn't slept last night.

"But the Apocalypse didn't come," President went on. "By the following year, we realized it was God's will that we instigate the Apocalypse ourselves, in order to make way for the Second Coming. Would anyone care for more toast?"

Teacher's shoulders jerked. "Who's *we*? You mean all the people who worked for you at the White House? Or you mean the Keepers of the Flame?"

"They were one and the same," President replied with a radiant smile.

Mommy could hardly taste the mango in her mouth. *Look, Princess! It says here President McDowell's giving a speech at the stadium tomorrow night.*

"Of course I only surrounded myself with people I could rely on."

You want to come with Daddy? Maybe we could get some seats up in the bleachers.

A breeze stirred Mommy's hair, which smelled musty from her pillow last night. She was suddenly aware of

President watching her. She held his gaze for a second and then turned away, heat rising in her cheeks. Down below, a pelican dove into the water and emerged with a fish whipping up and down in its beak.

"Why don't I show you around?" President said suddenly, putting both hands on the table. "I think you'll find Pisgah Island very . . . inspiring."

He smiled at Mommy and she felt another flush of discomfort and disgust. The woman thing she was doing—the bleeding—made her feel hot and sick to her stomach, especially when she remembered that it had to do with babies and getting married.

Hunter stood up with a loud scraping of his chair. "Yes, thank you, we'd all enjoy that very much."

The four of them followed President into the garden. The guards trailed behind at a discreet distance. Mommy glanced over her shoulder and saw that several seagulls had already descended on their table and were tearing pieces of toast out of the silver basket.

And then she saw something else, inside the house: the silhouette of a naked girl through a gauzy curtain. The girl appeared to be crying, covering her face with her hands. Mommy's heart lurched in her chest.

That's the First Lady in the picture, Princess. Isn't she pretty?

"This is where we lived while the virus was being released. After the cleansing was complete, I sent some of our Brothers and Sisters to establish an outpost, and they set up our settlement at the Crossroads. The rest of us stayed here to complete our work."

Not as pretty as your mom, of course. And there's the president's two boys.

"What work is that?" Cory burst out suddenly. She had been so quiet during breakfast that Mommy was startled by the sound of her voice.

"The Lord's work. The work of finding, or creating, the New Savior. Come this way. I'd like to show you the rose garden."

Off in the distance, through a grove of trees, Mommy could make out another house fenced in with trees and dense buttresses of shrubbery. It was smaller than the main house but bigger than their cottage. "Who lives there?" she asked President, pointing.

"That area is restricted. Ah, here we are!"

Mommy stared at the little house beyond the trees. She wasn't sure, but she thought she could hear the high-pitched cries of babies—lots of babies—coming from it. On the other hand, it might be goats. The cries sounded like the noises Nana's goats made.

"Notice the pale pink ones—they're a hybrid I created. I rather fancy myself an amateur scientist," President added.

"You're a *scientist*?" Teacher rasped. "Are *you* the one who made the Fire-us, then?"

"The . . . Fire-us? You mean the virus?" President bent down and plucked one of the pink roses. "I had quite a team of good biologists. They did their work well. Although there was a problem, as we all know. The virus was supposed to cleanse the entire world, rid it of sin and abomination. But due to an unforeseen technicality, it spared children. We had only tested it on healthy adults—having no idea it wouldn't harm children."

And grandmas, Mommy was about to add, but she bit her lip. She didn't want President to know about

Nana and the other old women at the Woods.

"Ironic, isn't it?" President continued with a laugh. "But that's just as well, because it brought you all here to Pisgah Island." He smiled at Mommy again and offered her the rose. "It's the same color as your blouse."

Mommy didn't want to touch the rose. She wanted nothing to do with President McDowell. But it seemed impolite to refuse, and in any case, she didn't want to get President angry. She took the rose and held it up to her face obediently. The fragrance was sweet, too sweet, and she felt briefly dizzy from it.

Mommy saw Hunter look at her, then at President, then at her again. "The Fire-us—I mean, the virus—is all gone now, though, right? Otherwise you all wouldn't be here."

"The original release has died out, yes," President replied. "Of course there is the second vial." He reached into the pocket of his blue jacket and pulled out a small glass tube stoppered with a cork. Inside the tube was a clear liquid.

Mommy dropped the rose. She felt Teacher grab her arm.

"No need to worry," President reassured them. "It's perfectly safe, as long as the stopper isn't removed or the vial doesn't break."

Mommy began to tremble all over. There it was: the Fire-us. *Is that all?* she wanted to say, staring at the clear liquid in the tiny glass tube. *Is that all it took to destroy the whole world? Destroy my First Mommy and First Daddy, all our First Mommies and First Daddies, and our brothers and sisters, too?*

She whirled around, wanting to scream, wanting to

thrash her arms out and hurt someone. Hurt *him*, this man, this monster. She clenched her hands into fists and bit down on her lower lip until she tasted blood.

Because how could she hurt him? He had *it*. He had a second vial. If anyone went near him, he could simply threaten to release it.

At last someone spoke. "W-what about the anecdote?" Teacher said shrilly. "Your good-bye-ologists made an anecdote, right?"

President smiled. "Antidote? There never was an antidote."

They climbed a grassy hillside. Daisies bobbed and danced in the breeze. From the top, Teacher could see the wide blue span of ocean that seemed to stretch on forever. For a moment, she imagined that they were all on vacation on a pretty island—her, Mommy, Hunter, and Cory—just a bunch of kids with this big, tall Grown-up who was maybe their rich uncle or a family friend.

But he wasn't. He was the Devil. The Book had taught them about Devils: *Resist the Devil, and he will flee from you. Your adversary, the Devil, as a roaring lion, walketh about, seeking whom he may devour. The New Jersey Devils massacred the New York Rangers 8–1.*

"Say no to drugs!" Teacher whispered.

"What did you say?" President frowned.

"I mean . . . how did all you Keepers survive, then, if there wasn't an antidote?"

"Ah! Well, let me show you."

He led them down the other side of the hill. Teacher was the only one who was talking now. Mommy, Hunter, and Cory had been very quiet, ever since President's announcement about there being no antidote. She didn't want to talk to him much, either, except that it was important to get all this Information. As soon as she was back in the cottage, she was going to get The Book out from where she'd hidden it behind an old dresser. The Keepers had tried to take The Book away from her once. They were not going to do it again.

When they got to the bottom, Teacher saw that there was a big, heavy-looking door on the side of the hill. "What's that?"

"A special bunker," President explained. "You see, Pisgah Island has been a presidential retreat for many years now. Like a vacation retreat," he added, reading the confusion on their faces. "The bunker was built in order to protect all presidents from nuclear attack, biological warfare, and so forth. Fortunately for us, in the Year 2002, it served to protect us from the virus so we could accomplish our great mission. We lived here for a week, until we were sure that the virus had burned itself out."

"How did you know when that was?" Teacher asked him.

"I sent volunteers out of the bunker. The first few died. The rest survived, so we knew we were fine. Shall we head back? I have a meeting at nine o'clock, and of course I must check on my bride. . . ."

Cory and Mommy both flinched at the word *bride*. Teacher followed President as he began sauntering back to the main house, his arms swinging at his sides. For a moment, she imagined that President was the important Grown-up she used to see on TV: giving speeches, shaking hands with foreign digging terries, signing treaties. He was so smooth, so self-assured . . . and yet this same Grown-up had murdered an entire world full of people.

Was he going to murder them, too?

"You must see this!"

President had stopped under a tree and was pointing to a nest that was cradled between two branches. Tiny gray heads poked out, their beaks snapping at the air.

"Baby ospreys!" President cried out. "Aren't they a miracle? *Life* is a miracle, isn't it?"

Behind her, Teacher could hear Hunter, Cory, and Mommy breathing hard.

"I think you're going to enjoy your time here at Pisgah Island," President said, regarding them. "You will be wonderful new additions to our family. Of course you must promise to abide by our laws and covenants. But once you know what they are, you will see—you will *truly understand*—why the Great Flame was necessary."

"But it's over, isn't it?" Hunter spoke up in a low, scared-sounding voice. "The Great Flame is over. So why do you keep the second vial of Fire-us, I mean the virus, around?"

President touched his pocket and pulled out the vial. Sunlight winked off the glass and broke into rainbow colors against his hand. "For resistors," he replied. "And now, I really *must* get back and check on my bride. Perhaps some of the Brothers and Sisters could see about getting you some more appropriate clothes. . . ."

Casting out sin . . . oh, I don't want to die . . . let him who is without sin cast the first stone . . . casting call from one to three looking for twins of all ages . . . and the

Lord was the word and the word was good . . . trust me, trust me, trust me . . . on your knees and pray . . . Annie get yer gun . . .

"We *gotta* get out of here."

"I am *not* going to become a Keeper."

"We *gotta* get that vial."

The four of them were talking a mile a minute as they stumbled back to their cottage. They had made their excuses to President McDowell: they were tired from their journey to Pisgah, they hadn't slept well last night, they needed naps, they would see about new clothes later. President had smiled his perfect smile at them, said "Of course," and disappeared in the direction of the main house. To his bride. Hunter still couldn't wrap his brain around that one: *bride*. Didn't President *have* a bride already? Weren't they someone's First Daddy and First Mommy? He seemed to remember something about that, from the Before Time.

A lizard skittered across the path. Overhead, palm fronds swayed in the breeze. There were no guards following them to the cottage. Hunter understood now that President expected the four of them to stay on Pisgah Island of their own free will. President had made it abundantly clear what happened to people who . . . well, *resisted*.

But what about the idea of a supersecret, predawn escape? What was the guard situation like then? Hunter would have to spend the next few nights assessing things. And in the meantime, he had to keep his family—keep Mommy and Cory and Teacher—safe from President. Until now, he had thought that Angerman was the craziest person in the world. Now, he realized that Angerman was a really Normal Guy compared to President.

"I wonder if the little ones are okay with Nana," Mommy murmured.

Hunter was about to reply when he spotted their cottage just ahead. He noticed with a start that the front door was wide open.

Teacher noticed it at the same time. She broke into a run. "The Book! They're looking for The Book!" she cried out.

"Where'd you hide it, Teacher?" Cory gasped.

"Behind the dresser. What if they found it?"

Just as the four of them reached the front door, Angerman came out of it.

He stopped when he saw them. "Good morning!" he said brightly.

Hunter resisted the impulse to smash Angerman in the mouth. Instead, he stepped forward and grabbed his arm and hissed, "What is going on? Why are you acting like one of them?"

"What were you doing in our cottage?" Teacher added, her eyes searching Angerman's baggy tunic to see if he was concealing The Book.

"I was sent to tell you there's a prayer meeting in one hour," Angerman explained. He shook Hunter's arm loose. "And now, if you'll excuse me—"

"I don't think so," Cory snapped. "Where is the gun, Angerman?"

Something flickered in Angerman's eyes. "Gun? What gun?"

"Nana's gun, jerk," Cory said with her jaw clenched. "The one you stole from her. The one we tried to get away from you yesterday. Give it back!"

Angerman smiled and shrugged. *"No habla Americano, scusi, per favore. . . ."*

Cory grabbed Bad Guy's head from where it lay on the step and shoved it right in Angerman's face. "Where—is—the—gun?" she shouted. *"Answer me!"*

Angerman's smile froze on his face. He gaped at Bad Guy, then at Cory. Then he let out a muffled cry and hurried off toward the main house.

Cory started after him but stopped when two Keeper men emerged from the woods. They called out to Angerman. The three of them continued on to the house.

Watching them, Cory sighed and swiped her hand across her brow. It left a streak of dirt and sweat on her skin, like war paint. Hunter stared at her in astonishment. Was this the same girl they had met at the Crossroads? The one who served food at the Food Court and wore wedding dresses and got bossed around by the Keeper women? For the first time that day, he felt the tiniest, tiniest shred of hope. Maybe he had an ally after all, one who could help him strategize a way out of this madness.

Chapter Thirteen

Teacher pushed past Cory and Hunter and strode into the cottage, her sneakers thumping on the wooden floor. In the blue bedroom, the bureau stood against the wall underneath a mildew stain on the wallpaper that looked like a hand with a pointing finger. Grunting, she shoved the chest of drawers away from the wall and then gasped with relief. The Book was right where she'd left it.

"Do you think he was looking for that?" Cory asked from the doorway. She jerked her head toward the front door. "Angerman?"

Teacher bent to retrieve The Book and caught a musty whiff of mildew. "I don't know. I don't think he's our enemy, but I'm still not sure we can trust him. I wouldn't want him to get his hands on this."

They walked into the living room, where Hunter and Mommy were sitting at opposite ends of the sofa. Everything was covered with a fine layer of dust and smudges of mildew, and the upholstery felt damp against Teacher's calves as she sat down in the squashy chair.

"I wonder how come they don't use this building?" Mommy spoke up. She leaned over the coffee table and blew a cloud of dust from the surface. "It must have been a pretty house."

"They probably have some kind of superstition about it," Hunter speculated. "Maybe they think it's cursed."

"*They're* cursed," Cory said under her breath.

Teacher shook her head. "Well, we're all living under a curse if we don't get that glass tube of Fire-us away from him."

The others looked at her, their faces filled with doubt and worry. "You mean . . ." Hunter began.

"We have to get rid of it somehow, destroy it so he can't ever set it loose again," Teacher said. She could feel her own heart rate speed up with anticipation and fear. "We have to steal it from him."

Cory slouched back in her chair, her chin sunk on her chest. She looked like a stone statue.

"Well?" Teacher asked, turning to Hunter and Mommy.

"You're right," Mommy said.

Hunter nodded. "I know—but here's the thing. What if Angerman goes after the guy first and breaks the bottle by accident?"

"We have to do it as soon as possible," Mommy said, her face white. "We need a plan to get it right away."

"Find Angerman, that should be our plan," Cory muttered. "First thing is to find him and tell him not to shoot Supreme Leader—President—whatever we're supposed to call him. Then we can come up with the perfect plan to grab the virus."

Mommy let out a shrill laugh. "Oh sure, we just have to explain things logically to Angerman. No problem! We'll just say, we know you've been looking for this guy for a long time to kill him, but now that you found him, don't do it, okay?"

"What else can we do?" Cory demanded.

"She's right," Teacher said. "We can't just go rushing

up to President and tell him to hand over the Fire-us. It's better if we give ourselves some time to plan."

Frowning, Mommy stood up and strode to the window. Hunter followed her with his eyes, Teacher noticed. For a moment she thought he was going to get up and join her at the window, but he didn't. Then, when Hunter found Teacher's eyes on him, he blushed and looked away.

"Can't you look at The Book or something?" he muttered.

"Okay." Teacher spread her hands over the cover, closing her eyes and trying to focus her thoughts. It never did any good to look at The Book for guidance when her mind was a whirlwind of scattered fears and worries. She took a deep breath, coughed at the mildew odor, and then exhaled in a long, steady stream.

Then she tilted The Book up onto its spine, and let it fall open. Teacher opened her eyes.

"What is it? What does it say?" Cory asked.

Teacher ran her finger down the pasted-in clippings. "It's from the yellow book. The yellow book code."

"What's that?" Cory asked, as Hunter and Mommy turned to listen.

"There was this big yellow book with a lot of numbers and names, which I don't know what they meant, and at the top of every page was a code, sometimes just one word but usually two words together. I can usually figure out what they mean. On this page here in The Book, I put in 'Safety—sandblasting, hardware—health, baby—bakers, fireworks—flight, voice—wallpaper, churches—clambakes,' and 'gift—glass.'"

Cory sat forward, elbows on knees. "But what does that mean? It doesn't make any sense."

"Well . . ." Teacher puzzled over the code, trying to let her mind make meaning out of the words. "There's a lot of things that are obvious, like safety, health, voice. Fireworks, that sounds like Fire-us to me—"

"Baby," Mommy broke in. She looked nervous. "What's baby bakers?"

Teacher ignored the question. She didn't want to think what baby bakers could mean. "I think what this whole message means is we have to get Angerman to hand over the gun—that's the hardware part—for our health. *Hardware—health.* That's pretty clear. And *gift—glass*, that could mean we need President to give us the glass bottle with the Fire-us, fireworks, flight—that could be something about a bird?"

"But what's the baby bakers part?" Mommy repeated.

Teacher swallowed. "I don't know," she admitted.

"But does The Book say that we will do it?" Cory asked. "Or just that we have to try?"

Teacher couldn't bring herself to say *I don't know* again. She closed The Book with a snap. "It doesn't matter. Remember the commandment, *Don't delay*. So, let's go."

Mommy led the way out the door, and paused for a moment to shield her eyes from the brilliant sunlight. "Let's split up," she suggested. "Whoever finds Angerman first has to get the gun away from him and explain about the bottle. Then we'll figure out the next step."

"I'll go with you," Cory offered. She pointed toward

the left. "I say we should start over there."

While Hunter and Teacher took off in the opposite direction, Mommy and Cory made their way along an overgrown path. Tendrils of creeping vine caught at their feet as they walked. Mommy paused to swat a thorny branch aside and Cory stepped past her, taking the lead.

"There's a building ahead," Cory said.

Mommy caught a faint mewing sound beneath the whispering of wind in the branches. She halted.

"Stop, Cory," she called out. "I heard something."

They paused, listening, and Mommy heard it again: the sound like a baby goat bleating for its mother.

"Did you hear it?" she whispered.

Cory looked back at her and nodded. "It's a baby."

The hairs on Mommy's arms stood up. "No, it's a baby goat."

"Come on."

Cory left the path, pushing through the dense shrubs and ducking under low branches. Mommy followed, making sure to be silent. In the spaces between leaves and branches, the wall of a house was visible, its clapboard siding warped and buckled from the sea air. The paint was peeling off in little flakes, giving the house a scabby, derelict look. Mommy realized with a tremor of surprise that this was the back of the building that President had said was off-limits. The two girls crept up to a thick oak tree and crouched behind it. A ground-floor window, open a crack at the bottom, looked out at their tree.

"You think Angerman is in there?" Mommy asked Cory, even though she was sure Cory didn't think so.

Cory didn't answer. She put her hand out to

Mommy's arm and gripped it.

The window was sliding up, and the fretful mewling of a baby sounded out loud and surprisingly close. Mommy stiffened.

While they watched, a girl not much older than Cory or Mommy, clutching a bundle to her chest, began climbing out the window. She hesitated, her legs dangling, and then jumped down, carefully cradling the bundle.

"What are you doing?" Cory asked in a low, clear voice.

The girl jerked as though shot, and looked around with wild eyes. The bundle of cloth she held to her chest let out a feeble wail. Mommy squeezed her eyes shut tight, and then looked again.

"Who are you?" the girl asked in a frightened whisper. She was pale, and her lank, stringy hair clung to her face as though she'd been sick in bed for many days. She swayed on her feet.

"We're not going to hurt you," Mommy said, stepping forward. She put out a gentle hand and moved the cloth away. A tiny, red-faced baby with tight-shut eyes raised trembling fists into the air. "Shh . . . don't fuss, little thing."

The girl backed up to the building, and cast a terrified look over her shoulder at the open window. "I wasn't—I mean—"

"Are you trying to run away?" Cory asked.

"Who are you?" the girl asked again, almost on the edge of tears.

"We're not from here," Mommy said. "Is this your baby?"

The girl ducked her face over the baby's, kissing its cheeks. She started to cry. "I don't want them to Test her. I thought I'd be happy to give her to them—it's supposed to be such an honor—but I know the babies never come back and I would miss her so much. I don't even get to see *him* anymore, and someone said he has a new bride—"

She broke off, unable to control her tears. Mommy put an arm across her shoulders and met Cory's eyes. This could have been Cory standing here.

"Is this *his* baby?" Cory asked. Everyone knew who *he* was.

"Y-yes." The girl sobbed.

"He marries all the girls and they all have babies," Cory said. "And they're all taken away for Testing and they never come back. Is that how it works?"

Mommy could feel the girl's shoulders jerking and quivering with anguish. She hugged the girl closer.

"Do any of the other men get married and have babies?" Cory went on. Her face was rigid with anger.

The girl raised a tear-streaked face, her mouth open. "No," she whispered.

"Leave her alone," Mommy warned Cory. "Can't you see she's—"

"Are *all* the babies *his* babies?" Cory pressed, her face fierce.

Mute, the girl nodded, and lowered her face to her baby's again.

"So you figured you'd just run away? How are you going to take care of that baby?" Cory blazed. "What if something happens to you? Did you *think* of that? Of who would take care of your baby if you *die*?"

"Cory, shut up!" Mommy gasped.

Trembling, Cory stepped back. The girl was crying silently into the baby's neck.

Mommy caught Cory's eyes. "What should we do?" she mouthed.

Cory didn't answer.

"Listen," Mommy said, trying to coax the girl back toward the house. "You're too weak to be running away. We'll come back later and help you, okay? Go back inside."

"All right," the girl said, obedient and meek.

Mommy held the infant while Cory gave the girl a hand climbing in through the window again. Tenderly, Mommy handed the swaddled baby back to the young mother. "What's your name?" Mommy asked.

"Esther 7:4," she whispered.

"We'll come back later, Esther," Mommy promised. "Your baby won't be tested."

She backed away from the window and joined Cory, who was pacing in a tight circle behind the oak tree. Mommy was shocked when she saw Cory's expression.

"What is it?" she asked. "Why were you so mean to her?"

Two red spots burned in Cory's cheeks, and her eyes were blazing. "Don't you see?" she asked, her voice harsh. "Puppy and Kitty. Ingrid. That girl's trying to do the same thing my sister did. President is their father."

Washed in the blood of the lamb . . . blood there will be blood I think there will be blood . . . look for sunny skies, temperatures in the high 80s . . . God help me . . . I don't think I can do this. . . .

* * *

Hunter scanned the beach from the dune. Nobody. Not even footprints. Teacher stood beside him, flipping through the pages of The Book and muttering in a low voice.

"Angerman isn't in *there*," Hunter said and began to lead the way down. "Come on—let's look over there."

A path was worn through the hummocks of bear grass and ropes of sea purslane that sprawled across the dune. As soon as Hunter stepped onto it, he could feel the difference between the soft sand and the hard-packed path. "They must use this trail a lot," he said, more to himself than to Teacher.

"We didn't come this way this morning," Teacher pointed out. "President didn't bring us this way."

"Then there's probably something here we're not supposed to see," Hunter guessed. He paused as a gull rose up squawking from the trail ahead of him. Then he went on, turning as the path switchbacked down the back of the dune. Below, he could make out an area sheltered from the ocean. There was a small building, the kind of thing that people used to have at the beach called cabanas. In front of it, there was a deep pit with sides reinforced by what looked like concrete blocks but which were blackened. The sand all around the pit was hard packed.

"What is that?" Teacher asked, standing beside him on the path and following his gaze down.

"I don't know." Hunter shook his head. In his mind he saw the image of burned forests, places where wildfires had scorched the land. They had passed many fire sites on their journey north. "Looks sort of burned, doesn't it?"

"Yes, it does." Teacher pushed ahead, sidestepping as the path grew steep.

Hunter glanced back over his shoulder as they slithered down the path. Down behind this dune, they were completely cut off from the rest of the island. He wondered why the Keepers had put this pit in this out-of-the-way spot if it was something they used regularly. And it had to be something they used regularly, because the path was well worn.

Ahead of him, Teacher was reaching for the door of the cabana. It opened outward, and Teacher poked her head inside. "Driftwood!" came her voice like a hollow echo. "Just a lot of wood. I guess they want to keep it dry."

Hunter walked to the side of the pit and looked down. The floor was sand mixed with ash, and there were small bits of charred wood. The smell of smoke was strong.

"Do you think they use it for cooking?" Teacher asked, rubbing her head in puzzlement.

"No. It's so far away from everything else," Hunter pointed out.

"Well, I don't know," Teacher said. She sounded annoyed, and she shifted the heavy Book from one arm to the other. She didn't like mysteries, Hunter knew. She liked things to be clear so she could decide if they should go into The Book or not. Hunter figured she also didn't like admitting when she didn't understand something.

"Whatever it is, Angerman isn't here," she said as she turned away. "Let's go. We've got to find him."

Chapter Fourteen

It wasn't until Teacher and Hunter were heading back toward their cottage that Teacher remembered about the prayer meeting. Angerman had mentioned it, just before Cory had scared him off with the mannequin head.

Teacher grabbed Hunter's arm and nodded at the meeting hall. "What about in there? Didn't Angerman tell us there was a prayer meeting thing this morning? Maybe *that's* where he is."

"You're right!" Hunter turned and began jogging toward the meeting hall.

"Unless he was just making that up!" Teacher called out.

"Yeah, well, you could be right about that, too!"

Teacher tucked The Book securely under her arm and sprinted after Hunter. When they reached the entrance, Teacher saw that the double doors were open a crack. From inside, she could hear the sound of President's deep, grown-up voice: "And the Lord spake unto Moses."

"By the Flame!"

"By the Flame!"

The building smelled faintly of horses and hay. Teacher had noticed it last night, during the wedding. *Wedding.* She squeezed her eyes shut and tried to block out the image of the terrified girl, who had worn the same kind of white dress Cory had worn back at the Crossroads.

"'Command the children of Israel, and say unto them, My offering, *and* my bread for my sacrifices made by fire, *for* a sweet savour unto me, shall ye observe to offer unto me in their due season.'"

"By the Flame!"

When Teacher opened her eyes again, she saw that Hunter was pressing his face against the double doors, one eye to the crack. "Is Angerman in there?" she whispered. "Do you see him?"

"Wait a sec—I'm looking."

The air was thick with heat. Cicadas hummed in the tall grass. Teacher glanced around, wondering where Mommy and Cory were. Maybe they'd found Angerman and intercepted him before the prayer meeting? In any case, she didn't see them. The main house and the grounds seemed to be empty. A few drops of water glinted in a white, bleached clamshell on the path.

"There he is!" Hunter whispered.

"Lemme see."

Hunter moved aside so Teacher could get up close. She peered through the crack. Several dozen Keepers occupied the rows of seats, men to one side, women to the other. President stood in front in the same spot where the old preacher man had stood last night. He held a brown leather book in his hands, open, and his face seemed to glow with fire as he read from it.

Teacher flinched at the sight of President's book. Instinctively, she curled her fingers under her left arm to make sure *her* Book was still there. It was.

And then she spotted Angerman. He was sitting right up front. For a brief second, Angerman turned his head to glance at a boy—maybe Teddy Bear's age?—who was squirming on a Keeper woman's lap. Teacher couldn't read Angerman's expression. Then he was facing forward again, listening with rapt attention to President's words.

Teacher frowned at the back of his head. "Now what do we do?" she said to Hunter. "Just wait and grab him on his way out?"

"I wonder if he's got the gun with him," Hunter mused.

Teacher gaped. "You don't think he'd be crazy enough to use it *now*, do you? With all those Keepers around?"

"He's crazy enough to do anything, Teacher. You know that." Hunter added, "Still, he'll probably wait till President's by himself. Better chance that way."

"Probably," Teacher agreed. The insect hum throbbed and pulsed with the heat. Teacher felt sweat slide down her spine.

Hunter peered through the crack again. "Let's just wait'll the prayer meeting's over. We can try to get him alone then."

Teacher felt The Book digging into her armpit. She pulled it out and regarded it for a second. She remembered its holy messages from before: *Safety—Sandblasting. Hardware—Health. Baby—Bakers.*

The messages tugged at her now. She sighed and let herself slide down onto the grass beside the building. She leaned against the wall and balanced The Book in her lap.

"What're you doing?" Hunter asked her.

"Consulting The Book."

"'And thou shalt say unto them, This *is* the offering

made by fire which ye shall offer unto the LORD; two lambs of the first year without spot day by day, for a continual burnt offering.'" President's voice rose to a muffled crescendo inside.

"So I've been thinking," Hunter said, sliding down next to Teacher. "First we gotta get Angerman and the gun and convince him to stay away from President, right? But then we gotta get the second vial of Fire-us and destroy it."

"I know, I know," Teacher said, frowning. She closed her eyes and ran her hand back and forth, back and forth across the cover of The Book. The whirr and buzz of insects grew louder and then faded. Her fingers lingered on the bumpy creases. "Nana said . . . what? The Fire-us needs a hostess—something like that. Without it, it'll burn itself out and die. So maybe we just need to bury the Fire-us deep in the ground."

"Not good enough," Hunter said, shaking his head. "What if it leaks out or something?"

Teacher let her fingers trail over the side of The Book; there was a damp spot from being under her armpit. Then she flipped it open. She blinked at the big black words that swam before her:

OUR SEMI-ANNUAL BED AND MATTRESS SALE!
QUEEN AND KING BEDS STARTING AT $259
BUNK BEDS STARTING AT $199
OUR PRICES CAN'T BE BEAT!

Teacher's heart thumped in her chest. *Bunk beds.* That had to be it.

"The bunker," she said out loud to Hunter. "Didn't President say the Keepers lived in the bunker while the Fire-us burned itself out?"

"Uh-huh." Hunter brushed an ant off his knee.

"So if the Fire-us can't leak into the bunker, that must mean it can't leak *out*, either."

"You mean . . . oh, *yeah*." Hunter began nodding very fast. "If we could put the vial in the bunker, then rig the bunker so that the vial would break right after we closed the door—"

"The Fire-us would be released inside the bunker with no one in it. Since it wouldn't have a hostess, it would burn itself out in a few days or a week or whatever," Teacher finished. "And then it would be gone from the world forever."

Hunter sat up very straight. His green eyes were flashing and his cheeks reddened. Teacher could tell that he was excited about their plan.

"We still gotta figure out how we're going to get the vial away from President," Teacher reminded him. "That's not gonna be easy."

"Maybe while he's sleeping."

"Or maybe we could trick him somehow."

The two of them fell silent. From inside the meeting hall came President's voice:

"'The one lamb shalt thou offer in the morning, and the other lamb shalt thou offer at even . . .'"

Teacher noticed just then that The Book was open to a different page. When had she turned the page? She didn't remember doing it.

The new page was a crazy jumble of words,

clippings, ads, scribblings. Teacher didn't recall ever seeing them before:

LEVIS 501 JEANS

Tomorrow is the last day to register for Professor Francis Galton's ceramics class at Ocala College. Hand-building and pottery wheel techniques. Raku and kiln.

Fort Lauderdale, City of the Sun!

When the clay goes into the kiln and undergoes the ordeal by fire, it comes out hard and perfect—a thing of beauty.

Send inquiries to the main office in Cold Spring Harbor, NY

New Atlantis Records presents . . .

~~EUGENE~~

EUGENICS

This is only a test.

Teacher touched the word *test* with her fingertip and the other words, too. She was about to read them out loud to Hunter when he cried out, "Hey!" and jumped to his feet.

"What?"

"There's Mommy and Cory."

Teacher squinted into the sun. The two girls were emerging from the woods, Mommy in front, Cory bringing up the rear. Cory had the mannequin head under her arm.

"Let's go tell 'em we've found Angerman," Hunter suggested. "Sounds like this prayer meeting's gonna be a little while longer."

"'kay." Teacher rose to her feet, her thoughts racing with the strange new words. *Kiln. Eugenics.*

* * *

A large brown beetle skittered across the path in front of Cory's feet. She had to resist the temptation to crush it. She felt as though her head was going to explode with rage. President and that girl. President and *all* those girls. President and Ingrid. President and *her,* almost.

On top of which, she had just figured out that President was the father of Ingrid's twins. Knowing this fact, this horrible fact, how could she go through with her plan to kill him? How could she *not* go through with it?

"There's Teacher and Hunter," Mommy said, breaking into her thoughts. "I don't see Angerman with them. I guess they didn't have any luck, either."

Cory looked up. Teacher and Hunter were coming toward them down the path.

She and Mommy hurried. The four of them met under a drooping palm tree and regarded each other breathlessly. It was as hot as an oven.

"Angerman's in the meeting hall," Hunter announced. "There's a prayer meeting going on. Plus, we found this weird shack on the beach with a big concrete hole next to it—"

"We found something, too," Mommy cut in, wiping her damp forehead. "There are other girls on the island. And babies!"

"What?" Teacher gasped.

Mommy proceeded to tell Teacher and Hunter about running into Esther 7:4 and her baby girl. When she got to the part about President and his "brides," Teacher's face turned ashy pale.

Hunter knotted his hands into fists. "Maybe Angerman's not so crazy after all, wanting to kill him.

McDowell is completely nuts."

"Mmm," Cory agreed.

A pair of yellow butterflies flitted through the air and landed on a plume of grass. Cory thought about all those babies not coming back, about Testing. Of *course* she had to kill President, even if he was Puppy and Kitty's father. How could she not? As long as he was alive, Puppy and Kitty—all the little ones—were in danger.

She sucked in a deep breath. "So Mommy and I figured it out. President is the father of all the babies on this island. The babies get taken away to be tested for some reason, and they never come back. And . . ." She hesitated. She could barely bring herself to say the words. "Puppy and Kitty . . ."

Teacher stared at her. "What about them?"

"President's their father, too," Cory blurted out.

"No way!" Hunter said.

Cory nodded. "It's the only explanation. President marries girls, and has babies with them, and then the babies get taken away for Testing. Whatever that is. Ingrid found out about that, and she didn't want her babies taken away from her. That's why she ran away with them."

"But maybe she married somebody else and not President," Teacher suggested feebly.

"I'm sure it was President," Cory insisted. "I remember when Ingrid got fitted for a wedding dress at Danielle's Bridal Shoppe, and then the Keepers took her somewhere. She was gone for a long time. When she came back, her stomach started getting big. And then the twins were born."

"Danielle's Bridal Shoppe?" Teacher repeated.

"That's where *your* dress was from, Cory. Does that mean you were supposed to marry—"

"Yup. And I bet after Ingrid ran away, that's when they started bringing the girls here and keeping them here until they had their babies. None of them ever go back to the Crossroads, anyway."

They all let that sink in for a moment. Then Mommy grabbed Cory's arm. "Cory, you've gotta get out of here right away. What if they recognize you? They'll make you marry him."

"No way!" Cory spat on the ground. "I will never marry him, *never.* I would rather *die* first."

A small deer emerged from a clearing in the woods, froze, then bounded away. Cory felt the hard, round head of the mannequin pressing into her side. She wasn't sure why she kept carrying it around with her. For some odd reason, she found it comforting, as if it promised her she would really hold the severed head of her enemy. She would kill him. She didn't care what it took.

"So what do we do?" Teacher said after a moment. She leaned against a tree and hugged The Book to her chest.

"It's still the same plan," Hunter explained. "We've gotta get Angerman alone and talk to him, keep him from going loco and messing everything up. Then we've gotta get that vial away from President. Teacher and I had an idea," he said, turning to Cory and Mommy. "If we rig the bunker somehow, we can stash the vial in the bunker and slam the door shut so that the vial breaks. The Fire-us will be released with no one in there. It'll burn itself out after a while, like Nana said."

"What a good idea!" Mommy cried out.

Then something occurred to Cory. "Hunter. Did you say you and Teacher found some weird shack?"

Hunter pointed in the direction of the beach. "Uh-huh. Over there. We couldn't figure out what it was for. But we got the feeling that we weren't supposed to be there."

"Is it far away?" Cory asked him. "Could we check it out?"

Hunter glanced across the lawn at the meeting hall. The doors were still closed and the drone of President's voice still rose and fell with the chirring of insects. "I guess so, as long as we come right back."

They started through the woods, with Hunter in the lead. Teacher slowed her steps until she was walking side by side with Cory.

"Why do you want to see it?" Teacher asked her. "The shack, I mean."

"I don't know," Cory said, shrugging. "Maybe it's President's secret hiding place or something. Maybe it'll give us some clues about how we can get the vial away from him."

"That's an excellent point," Hunter called over his shoulder. "That's a *really* excellent point."

After a few minutes, the path ended, and they came upon a clearing. Beyond a sandy rise of dune, Cory saw blue water, waves, sky. In her mind she pictured Puppy and Kitty racing up the dune, yelling "Beach!" like she used to do with Ingrid years ago. She wondered if the twins were happy back at the Woods, with Nana and the other grandmas. She wondered if they missed her as desperately as she missed them. For a moment, she felt an ache like a knife in her side. Then she shook it off.

They took a zigzaggy path up and over the dune. Down below, Cory spotted the shack. It was built of wood and had a sagging door.

When they got to the shack, Cory looked inside. Except for some driftwood, it was completely bare. An old sun-bleached poster was pinned to the wall. There were some words on it—WATER SAFETY RULES—and below that, a drawing of a person's head and arms, and nothing else. The rest of the person's body, and all the other words on the poster, had faded away.

In front of the shack was a deep, blackened pit with straight sides. Cracks ran along the walls in crooked lines, like lightning bolts. Cory winced at the strong smell of smoke. "What do you suppose they use that for?" she asked the others.

"You think it's another book-burning place? Like back at the Crossroads?" Mommy suggested.

"Doesn't smell like books," Cory replied. She stood on the edge of the pit and looked inside. It was full of charred wood and ashes. A breeze made a small dust devil, uncovering a lump.

Sunlight picked out the thing deep inside the pit: some object. Cory squinted and stared.

And stared.

It was a small skull.

Cory felt bile rise in her throat. "Guys . . ."

"What is it?" Mommy demanded.

Cory pointed. Mommy saw, and then Hunter and Teacher, too.

"Trial by fire," Teacher announced in a trembling voice. "This is a kiln. This is the Testing place. The Book told us this."

"What?" Hunter demanded. "What are you talking about, Teacher? What kill?"

"The *kiln*," Teacher repeated, sounding more hysterical. "Don't you see? This is the Testing place."

"Baby bakers," Cory whispered. She glanced at the head in her arms, and then at the little skull again.

Mommy clasped her hand over her mouth and began screaming.

Chapter Fifteen

Hunter put his arm around Mommy's shoulders and dragged her away; the harsh sound of her sobs drowned out the hammering in his own ears. They stumbled in the heavy sand. He knew Cory and Teacher were following, and he had a vague idea that the ocean was in front of them, but his eyes were blurred—as if he'd lost his glasses. He blinked tears away.

"Why?" Mommy cried over and over. "Why? He's insane. He must be completely insane."

A strong breeze buffeted them as they staggered out from the shelter of the dune onto the beach. The gust lifted Hunter's bangs and then flattened them on his sweaty forehead again, and he was suddenly aware that he was standing with his arm around Mommy. He stepped away, almost tripping in his haste, and shoved his hands into his pockets.

The four of them stood on the sand, isolated from one another, sick and speechless. Hunter felt a fresh wave of powerlessness every time a wave crashed onto the beach in front of him. What could he do? He wasn't old enough or smart enough or brave enough, he thought with mounting dismay. How could he do anything against such a terrible Grown-up? A Grown-up who wasn't content to kill off all the big people, but had to kill little children, too. What could he possibly do against something that bad?

A broad, wet, shining ribbon of sand stretched around the island, a low-tide flat where plovers ran back and forth on skinny yellow legs and poked their sharp bills downward. And beyond was the sea, going out and out to join the sky. Hunter knew the sea didn't care if President McDowell had wiped out most of the human race. And he knew the sea wouldn't care when the last human being fell—whether it was Mommy or Action Figure or Hunter himself—any of them. The birds would still scurry back and forth, just out of reach of the lapping surf, and the sun would still go down and then come up again. Hunter wished he hadn't let go of Mommy. Even just touching her hand would be enough to reassure him that they were still real and still on earth. He wanted to cry.

"There's Angerman," Cory spoke up.

Hunter gulped back tears as they all turned to watch Angerman make his way toward them across the beach. The wind tossed his dark hair around his head and pressed his shirt against his body. He raised a hand in greeting and jogged the last few yards.

"This is a gloomy-looking group," he said.

None of them spoke. Hunter noticed Cory shift Bad Guy under her arm, as though preparing to confront Angerman with the head. He stepped forward to cut her off.

"Listen," Hunter spoke up. His voice shook, and he made himself stern. "We know you want to kill President, but there's something you have to know."

He paused, bracing himself for any kind of weird reaction from Angerman, but nothing happened. The other boy just looked at him, his eyebrows in a slight arch as if inviting Hunter to continue.

"He's got more Fire—more virus; he carries it around with him," Hunter continued. "All this—Testing—this terrible stuff the Keepers do—they only do it because they're afraid of him."

"How do you know?" Teacher broke in.

He glanced back at her. "I don't, not for sure. But if we destroy the second bottle of virus, I bet these people would all just leave or ignore the guy or whatever."

"And they wouldn't do any more Testing?" Mommy asked, her voice quavering.

Hunter shrugged and turned back to Angerman. "All I know is, if you shoot President with the gun, you might break that glass bottle by accident and release Fire-us again and we'll die. We have to get it away from him before anything else—we have to get it and destroy it in a way that won't hurt anyone. So keep away from him," he finished, lifting his chin in defiance.

Angerman nodded. "I see what you mean."

The reasonableness of his voice was almost as shocking as anything else Angerman had ever said or done. The wildness, the rage, the irrational outbursts: it was as if none of that had ever happened. Angerman rubbed his chin and looked out at the breaking waves.

"Right," he said with a firm nod of his head. "Gun breaks glass, virus kills all, ergo no bang-bang."

"You could throw the gun into the water," Mommy said, taking a step toward him. "'Killing Is Wrong. Vote for Death Penalty Reform.'"

"Okay, Mommy." Angerman gave her a sweet smile that made Hunter clench his fists by his sides. "Okay."

They began walking along the wet sand, back toward

the compound. The birds raced along in front of them, always keeping just out of reach, one eye on the kids, one eye on the advancing waves. Hunter shaded his eyes as they walked into the path of the sun.

Cory hitched the head up higher under her arm, angling it toward Angerman. "Are you really going to throw the gun in the water?"

"I'll get rid of it," Angerman said with a dismissive wave of his hand. The head didn't seem to have any effect on him whatsoever. "Now, about the vial. I'll have to get it for you."

Teacher frowned. "Huh?"

"Trust me," Angerman said. "I can get it."

Hunter exchanged a doubtful glance with Teacher, but this was not the time to argue. If the guy was being cooperative, they had to *Just Do It*.

"Okay," Hunter said, hoping his voice didn't sound too skeptical. He tried to keep the memory of the kiln from sidetracking him. "We had this idea that we could take it to the bunker, and maybe like throw it inside and slam the door shut—you know, so it would break open and then just catch on fire—"

"Burn out," Teacher corrected him.

"Right." Hunter nodded. "So that's where we should meet and we'll—we'll take care of it."

"Okeydokey. When the dinner bell rings, don't go to eat. Meet me at the bunker, and I'll have the virus." Angerman halted, turned, and raised both hands toward them in a gesture of benediction. "Go forth and have no fear," he said, and then walked away.

The others stood watching him, not speaking until he was out of sight.

"I don't know . . ." Teacher began.

"Is he really okay now or is he just faking?" Mommy wondered aloud.

Hunter didn't volunteer an opinion. He felt far less confident than he had let on, but he didn't see what choice they had. With a sigh, he looked back the way they had come. Already, the incoming tide had erased their footprints from the beach.

As if they'd never existed at all.

Mommy trudged through the hot sand, each footstep heavier than the last. From the corner of her eye, she caught a flicker of movement and a high shrill cry of a bird that sounded like one of the little children, and for an instant she felt her heart constrict—Baby was running barefoot and laughing, or was it Doll or one of the twins? She dropped her gaze to the path, trying to focus her thoughts and put them in order.

Get the vial. Destroy the virus. Eliminate the president's hold over his people.

But most of all, don't think about the kiln.

With relief, she stepped up onto the worn boardwalk that marked the beginning of the formal pathway through the compound. Their feet clunked and thunked on the boards. Teacher and Hunter were talking in low voices behind her, and in front, Cory was walking with long strides, silent and straight backed. From around the compound came the sound of voices and doors opening and shutting, but Mommy willed herself to tune it all out, to imagine herself in a place that had no Keepers in it. But a gasp from Cory snapped her to attention.

At the same instant, she heard hoofbeats and the

familiar rattling of chariot wheels. Cory froze, and Mommy stopped short to keep from bumping into her. What Mommy saw over Cory's shoulder almost made her heart stop: chariots, men on horses, and a golf cart with the Woods emblazoned on the side, Nana at the wheel.

And all the children riding along with her.

"No!" Cory whispered.

"Mommy! Mommy!" came a shout of joy, and Baby jumped from the cart and was running toward them, Doll hot on her heels.

Mommy felt as though something inside her was trying to jump out of her body, the old screaming spirit that raged and burned. "No!" she shrieked, putting up her hands and backing away. "NO!"

Then Kitty and Puppy were tumbling out of the cart, running with open arms toward Cory. Teddy Bear and Action Figure began running, too.

Mommy and Cory stood as though turned to stone, while the little children jumped around them like crickets, clamoring and grabbing and talking all at once.

"There she is!" a man shouted. "That's Corinthians 1:19!"

Deuteronomy 29:28 stood up in the stirrups on the horse he was riding and pointed at Cory. Beside him, President McDowell sent the group of kids a pleased and startled look, and then let out a laugh.

"Why did you do it?" Hunter shouted at Nana. "How could you bring the children here?"

Nana was slumped behind the steering wheel of the golf cart, her face lined with worry. "I—why—they threatened—were going to kill my mother—" she broke off. Her eyes pleaded. "And they promised the children would be safe here."

Mommy saw Deuteronomy 29:28 point at Puppy and Kitty. Two men approached.

Frantic, Mommy grabbed Puppy and Kitty by the arms and began to run back toward the beach, dragging the children with her. Her breath came in gulps; she stared wide-eyed at the sky, and then the men caught them, scooping Puppy and Kitty up into their arms. The children screeched and struggled, and Mommy fell to her hands and knees, too stunned to make a sound.

"What are you doing!" Nana cried out in horror. "You promised!"

"We'll have a Testing tomorrow," came President's voice from far away, "but tonight—tonight we'll have a wedding."

Panting like a beaten dog, Mommy turned around and saw President McDowell remove the soldier's hat from Cory's head and tip her face up.

"Let's not delay any longer, shall we?" he said, and smiled a glittering smile.

Chapter Sixteen

Puppy and Kitty screamed and sobbed as the guards took them away. Baby, Doll, and Teddy Bear began crying. Action Figure grabbed a large stick from the ground and started after the guards.

"Killum!" he announced, waving the stick in the air. "Die, bam-bam!"

Hunter grabbed his brother's arm and yanked him back. "Action, *no*!"

Cory had to summon all her strength not to hit President with the mannequin head. *You monster, you baby murderer, you Satan!* She wanted to spit at him, claw his eyes out. But instead she balled her fists so tightly that her nails tore into her palms. She willed her mouth to smile, one twitching, trembling lip at a time. She willed herself to meet President's gaze, even though all she could see was the ghost image of the twins thrashing and struggling in the arms of the guards.

They had been looking at *her*—not at Mommy—pleading for help. They knew she was the strong one. She had to be strong now.

President turned her soldier's hat over in his hands and regarded her shorn hair. She nodded quickly in the direction of the twins. "Is that necessary?" she said in a light, friendly voice. "If you let them spend the night with us tonight, they'll be easier to handle tomorrow."

"They'll be just fine," President said. He cocked his

head. "So you are Corinthians 1:19. I had heard that you had very long hair, like your sister. You must have cut it recently."

At the mention of Ingrid, heat rose to her cheeks. "It was bothering me," she replied. "It was so hot."

"Well, you're still a very pretty girl," President said. "Tall for your age, aren't you? I hope Ephesians 5:6's wedding dress will fit you. There's no time to get another one."

"How did you find them?" Hunter demanded. "The little kids, I mean—and Nana."

"Your golf carts," President explained.

Cory glanced over at Nana, who was sitting in the golf cart with her head in her hands. Her shoulders were shaking and shuddering. Cory realized that she was crying.

It seemed hopeless. There they were: her, Hunter, Teacher, and the little ones . . . Mommy, who was still on the ground on her hands and knees, speechless with grief . . . Nana in the golf cart, useless . . . surrounded by President and Deuteronomy 29:28 and dozens of Keeper guards with spears. What could they—what could *she*—possibly do to stop Puppy and Kitty from being tested in the morning? There was also the vial of Fire-us, which they had to get away from President. She would kill him right here and now, if she could, except that Angerman—wherever he was—had the gun. She had to think.

A small brown sparrow lit on the ground, pecked at something, and flitted away. Cory watched it go. It disappeared into the sky, which was white and hazy with the noon sun. The day was half gone already. So little time.

"The wedding ceremony will take place after

dinner," President announced. "Deuteronomy 29:28 will officiate."

"By the Flame," Deuteronomy 29:28 said, bowing his head.

Hunter stepped forward. "Cory can't marry you, she's a girl! Besides, you already have a bride," he rasped.

President's eyes flickered with amusement as they regarded Hunter. "Please refer to her by her proper name, Corinthians 1:19. As for Ephesians 5:6—she has served her purpose."

Cory's mind flashed to Effie in her wedding dress, looking terrified as she went off with President. *It is my wedding night,* President had told them. What exactly did that mean, *wedding night*? Was that what Nana had told them about the other day? Males putting their sperms inside females who had started the Curse? And then, months later, the females getting big stomachs and having babies? It sounded ridiculous, but nobody seemed to think it was a joke.

Ruth 2:10 and Proverbs 3:21 and the other women at the Crossroads had prepared Cory for the wedding itself. They had fussed over her long white dress, pinning and sewing, and chattered to her endlessly about the ceremony, the beautiful vows, the honor of being Chosen.

But they had not prepared her for this wedding-night business. They had not said a word about it. Cory closed her eyes and tried to recall her Visioning. The stony path. Trying to find her way. The owl saying to her, "Take off the veil." But nothing about a wedding night.

Cory opened her eyes and met President's. He was smiling at her, and his smile was not kind.

She was not ready for this.

She *had* to be ready for this.

She put her hand on President's arm, the way she used to see Ingrid do with boys a long, long time ago. She flicked her tongue across her lips. They were cracked and salty tasting.

"This is such an honor," she said in a honey-sweet voice. "I can't wait for tonight."

"Cory!"

Mommy, who had been in some sort of trance, leaped to her feet. Baby, Doll, and Teddy Bear swarmed around her legs, sputtering and crying and calling out her name.

"Cory, you *can't*!" Mommy shouted.

"That's Corinthians 1:19, and of course she can," President told her with a smile.

Cory ignored Mommy. She couldn't explain to her or Hunter or Teacher that the only way she could keep Puppy and Kitty from getting tested tomorrow morning was to get President alone tonight. She felt her pocket for her knife, but it was gone, lost.

"I have to go get ready now," she told President.

"The women will help you, Corinthians 1:19," President said. "You must be bathed and shaved. Perhaps they can do something with your hair."

"Cory!" Mommy repeated.

President's smile faded. "That's *Corinthians 1:19.* You are not a very obedient girl, are you?"

Hunter stepped forward and pulled Mommy away. "Don't say anything else," he hissed.

Cory moved closer to President and squeezed his arm. She didn't want his attention on Mommy. "I'll see you tonight," she whispered.

President nodded distractedly. "Yes. Tonight."

As Cory pulled her hand away from his shirtsleeve, she noticed that her torn palm had left a bloody imprint on the white fabric. She turned and headed for the main house, her head spinning and her heart hammering in her chest.

She had to find the gun. And then she would get ready for President's last wedding night.

"I always knew that girl was crazy," Teacher said to Mommy and Hunter. "I was right after all!"

Teacher, Hunter, and Mommy had snuck into the main house. It had been Hunter's idea, so they could scrounge around and look for something to rig up the bunker door. President was at a meeting with Deuteronomy 29:28 and the other Keepers. Teacher wasn't sure how long the meeting would last.

"Never mind about Cory," Hunter snapped. "We've gotta find the stuff for the bunker. If we don't stop President tonight, he's gonna test Puppy and Kitty tomorrow."

"Don't *say* that!" Mommy cried out. "Don't say that, Hunter, please don't say that anymore!"

Teacher hugged The Book to her chest. The front hallway was deserted. Above an antique wooden table hung a framed drawing of a very young boy. Or was it a girl? The drawing was so faded and stained with damp, it was hard to make out the features.

Seeing the drawing, Teacher's thoughts flashed to Teddy Bear. She wondered how he was doing. A gray-haired Keeper woman—the one who had served them breakfast this morning—had taken him, Baby, Doll, and

Action Figure to a special cabin for naps.

Teacher doubted that any of the children would be able to sleep. Although she knew that sometimes, when Teddy Bear was scared, he closed his eyes and kind of passed out. Her chest tightened at the thought of him so terrified, so alone.

She turned abruptly to Hunter. "What are we looking for, exactly?"

"Maybe some rope and something long and elastic, like a bungee cord," Hunter replied. "I don't know. I haven't quite got this figured out."

A door opened and shut, startling the three of them into silence. Teacher whirled around and realized that it was just the wind making the screen door swing back and forth. The Keepers had vanished; the house was silent and still.

"Guys, it's okay," she whispered. "But we should try to be quieter. I think Cory might be upstairs with some Keeper women. You know, getting ready for the . . . the . . ." Her voice trailed off.

"You think Angerman's really gonna meet us at the bunker with the vial, like he promised?" Mommy whispered to Hunter.

"He has to. It's our only chance."

The three of them proceeded down the hall. The inside of the house smelled old, mildewy, damp. Brown stains bloomed across the cream-colored wallpaper. They reminded Teacher of continents on a map: Europea, Chinesia, Antafrica. The names didn't sound right, but her thoughts were too scattered to remember them.

Hunter started opening and closing drawers,

cabinets, closet doors. He called out the results of his search as he went along. "Nothing. Some coats, boots, hats. Paper clips. Books. Nothing. Nothing here."

"Books?" Teacher clasped The Book tightly and rushed up to him.

"Not now, Teacher," Mommy told her. "We may not have a lot of time."

"Yeah. All right."

They went into another room. It looked like some sort of living room. There was a long cream-colored couch with pale pink roses on it, some white wicker tables, and a wooden bookcase.

Teacher's eyes darted to the bookcase. There was a framed photograph, and that was it. No books.

Hunter looked under the cushions of the couch and under the tables. He tugged on the cords of the window shades. "Not exactly right," he announced, looking frustrated.

"Why can't we use them?" Mommy asked him.

"I don't know. They're not exactly right. I don't know."

Hunter crossed his arms over his chest. Teacher was surprised to see that his eyes were shiny with tears.

Mommy saw it, too. She put her hand on Hunter's arm. "Don't worry. We'll figure it out," she whispered.

He stared at her hand as if it would burn him. But he didn't pull away. "Why should we figure it out?" he said, his voice cracking. "Why is it up to us to save the world? We don't know anything. We shouldn't *have* to know anything. We're just kids!"

"Hunter," Teacher said, trying to sound reasonable. "Perhaps this is a good moment to consult The Book."

"How can The Book help us now?" Hunter cried out. "Cory's about to get married to the President of the United States, who murders kids and who has a vial of Fire-us in his pocket. Angerman's running around with a gun. We're all prisoners here, and there are no Grown-ups who can help us. Not even Nana. What does The Book have to say about all *that*, Teacher?"

Before Teacher could reply, Hunter picked up the photograph from the bookcase. It was a picture of President, smiling and waving at an invisible crowd. Hunter dropped it on the floor and ground his shoe into it. The glass splintered and cracked.

"Hunter, what are you doing?" Mommy gasped.

Teacher went over to where Hunter stood and picked up the frame. It came apart in her hands. Pieces of wood and broken glass cascaded to the ground.

And then she noticed something. There was another picture under the picture of President.

Very carefully, she peeled away the old photograph, which was scratched and smeared with dirt from Hunter's shoe.

Underneath was a family portrait. Teacher could tell that it was from the Before Time. There was President in a suit. Next to him was a very pretty woman with dark, curly hair. The words came to Teacher from her back memory: *First Lady*.

Sitting in front of them were two boys. One of them appeared to be nine or ten. The other one was older . . . Teacher's heart hammered violently.

"Guys!" Teacher shrieked. "This is *Angerman*!"

"What?"

Hunter and Mommy gathered on either side of

Teacher and studied the photograph. Teacher pointed to the older boy. He looked almost exactly like Angerman, except that his hair was short. He was wearing a navy blue jacket and a crisp-looking white shirt. "See? It's him!"

"There's no way," Mommy said, shaking her head. "This picture is from the Before Time. This boy would be, like, a Grown-up now."

"Yeah, but it looks just like him," Teacher insisted.

Mommy shrugged. "But it can't be. Wait—" She pointed to the younger boy. "Look at *him*, though."

The only sound was Teacher's ragged breathing. She looked at Mommy—her eyes were widening with astonishment.

"Oh—oh—" Mommy stammered. "*This* is him."

Teacher sucked in a deep breath and nodded. Mommy was right. The younger boy could easily be Angerman about five years ago.

The photograph shook as Teacher turned it over in her hand. In someone's delicate, flowery handwriting were the words:

COLIN, MARY, SAM & DAVID

PISGAH

JANUARY 2002

Teacher, Hunter, and Mommy began talking at once.

"David! That's what Mrs. Johnson called Angerman back at the Woods."

"Sam must be his brother. Where is he, then?"

"Where's this First Lady named Mary? Is she his First Mommy?"

"How did Angerman find us in Lazarus?"

"Guys!" Teacher clasped her hand over her mouth. "Do you know what this means?"

Mommy let out a sob and nodded. "President is Angerman's father."

Chapter Seventeen

Cory glanced over her shoulder, and when she saw there was nobody in sight down the hallway, she opened the bedroom door and stepped inside without a sound. Getting away from the women had been simple, really. "A chance to find my Visioning again to make sure my heart is pure," had sounded like such a logical—or Keeper-of-the-Flame logical—request. And she had fooled them from top to bottom into thinking she wanted to be married to President, all that eyelash flapping and looking shy and excited. Her Visioning was crystal clear already: she was going to kill President tonight, his very last wedding night. A sneer of contempt curled her lip as she pushed the door shut and looked around.

Could this be the room Angerman had been sleeping in? None of the rooms she had tried so far showed any trace of him, and she was running out of time. Frowning, Cory studied each corner of the room from where she was standing, trying not to rush, knowing she was in a desperate rush. From underneath the bed, a corner of something wooden was peeking out. The picture frame. The stupid picture frame. Cory knelt by the bed and reached under. It was Angerman's empty frame that he used for his TV speeches. This was his room.

Now Cory flung herself flat out on the floor to peer

under the bed. Balls of dust. A pencil. A dead, curled-up bumblebee. No gun.

She vaulted upright, then heaved the mattress aside. She yanked the drawers out of the dresser and swept all the knickknacks off the shelves. No gun. Nothing. Cory clenched her fists. He must still have it with him. He wouldn't dare hide it someplace that one of the Keepers could find it, would he? He would throw it in the ocean, hide it in his room, or have it with him.

If it wasn't in his room, he had it with him.

Because Cory knew he wouldn't throw it in the ocean. He wanted to kill President just as much as she did. He didn't fool her for a second, promising to get rid of the gun. He was planning to use it.

But Cory couldn't take the chance that he would fail, or that he wouldn't kill President in time. Tomorrow Kitty and Puppy would be tested, unless President were killed *tonight*. It had to be tonight.

Fighting down a groan of frustration, Cory twitched the curtains aside and looked out. Below, she could see Puppy and Kitty and the other children huddled together, being spoken to by Deuteronomy 29:28. They clutched one another, their faces a picture of woe in the late afternoon light. The curtain rod creaked as Cory pulled on the fabric, crushing it into a ball in her fist. For a long, anguished minute, she stared out the window at her niece and nephew. Then she turned away, her eyes burning with tears.

She didn't believe she would ever see them again, because she didn't think she would survive the night. She didn't need a Visioning to tell her she was going to kill

President, but she could imagine nothing for herself beyond that, no life after tonight. She crossed the room in three quick strides and went out, searching for Angerman and the gun. The day was running out.

Hunter had bitten his nails down so far they were stinging and raw. He picked through the odd assortment of twine and gift-wrapping ribbon and waistband elastic they had gathered and brought to their bungalow, turning them over and over. But his mind kept going blank. Think. *Think.* They had to come up with a way to release the Fire-us inside the bunker, some way that was safe, that nobody would be exposed, so that President wouldn't have any power over them anymore. A way to rig up the door, then get the vial inside, and then—

But every time Hunter tried to concentrate on a plan, he thought about Angerman being President's son, and his thoughts would go spinning off into a hundred different directions. Had Angerman known all along? Did he guess? Was he faking being crazy or was he really crazy in the same way President was? Because the president was sure crazy. Could you get that sort of thing from your father in your jeans, hand-me-down blue jeans? What could he, Hunter, have gotten from *his* father? Where was Angerman's First Mommy Lady?

Across the room, Mommy was sorting through the contents of a toolbox she had found under the kitchen sink. A rusty hammer. Three different kinds of screwdrivers. A knife with a retractable blade. She kept pawing through them, taking them out, putting them back. They clanked and scraped against the metal toolbox, setting Hunter's teeth on edge.

"I'm trying to think!" he blurted out.

Mommy stared at him, still holding the hammer in one hand. Her eyes were red with crying. "It's almost time." Her voice was hollow.

"I know, I know." He tossed the twine aside, and from the corner of his eye, he saw through the window that the shadows of the trees were getting long. "Where's Teacher?"

"I'm in here," came Teacher's voice from one of the bedrooms.

She came out, a deep crease in her forehead. She was carrying The Book open in front of her like a tray.

Hunter watched her, while a nagging worry began to fight with hope. She had the strangest look on her face, as though she had discovered something new and surprising in The Book. "Did you think of something?" he asked.

For a moment she didn't answer. Still holding the hammer, Mommy stepped away from the kitchen counter, her eyes on Teacher. Nobody spoke, and just then, they heard the clanging of the dinner bell. Hunter's heart stumbled and raced. Mommy let out a stifled whimper.

"I think I know how to do it," Teacher finally said.

"What? How?" Hunter and Mommy said at once.

Teacher's head was bent over the pages, and her voice was muffled as she read Nana's explanation aloud, "*'Children don't get the Fire-us because they don't have the hormones until pew-bertie.'*"

"Right? So?" Hunter urged. He could see people—Keepers—walking toward the main house for dinner.

Angerman should be on his way to the bunker. Did he get the Fire-us from President? How could he? What if he—

"So I don't have pew-bertie yet," Teacher said.

Mommy's face reddened. "But—"

"I can take the bottle of Fire-us into the bunker and open it up," Teacher said. "It won't make me sick. After a couple of days it will be all burned up, right? That's what Nana said. If it doesn't have a body to go into it burns up."

Hunter couldn't speak. He couldn't make any sound come out of his throat. The dinner bell clanged again. Why hadn't he thought of it? But he wasn't sure if he had pew-bertie himself. Nana had explained: there were things about his voice, and hair, and the thing in his throat. His head was spinning. His throat felt swollen and tight. He thought he had it but maybe not. But how could he be sure if—

"No," Mommy said. Tears welled up and spilled onto her cheeks. "No, it's too dangerous!"

"No it's not," Teacher said. Gently, she closed The Book and laid it on a chair. "And anyway, it's too late to think up anything else."

Nobody spoke. Teacher looked from Mommy to Hunter, and she looked scared. *"Right?"*

At last, Hunter forced himself to speak. "She's right," he croaked. "We gotta go *now*. Angerman should be on his way to the bunker right now."

"Teacher!" Mommy wailed. Then turned and flung the hammer across the room with a cry of anger. It smashed against the wall, leaving a hole that rained dust. She hurried toward the door. "Oh, come on!"

They sprinted out of the bungalow, keeping to the shadows of the overgrown path—Mommy, followed by Teacher, with Hunter bringing up the rear. He could hear Teacher muttering to herself as they half ran, half walked toward the beach.

"It won't hurt me. I'll be okay. Don't worry, Teddy. Don't be scared. Don't be scared."

Dried leaves crunched under their feet. A startled bird burst out of the underbrush and flew off, chattering, and Hunter's thoughts skittered away to Angerman again. They would have to tell him about President. That was the sort of thing a person had to know. But what if Angerman went blundering off in a fury before they could—before *Teacher* could take care of the Fire-us? Did Angerman have pew-bertie? What if Angerman didn't want to go along with the plan once he found out who President was?

"Teacher," he called in a hoarse whisper. "Maybe we shouldn't tell Angerman about that picture we found until later—you know, afterward."

Teacher looked back at him. She seemed to understand what he meant, because she nodded. "Good idea."

Then Teacher turned and walked into Mommy. Teacher bit back a yelp.

"What is it?" Hunter asked.

Mommy was standing at a bend in the path, where the view to the beach opened up. Silent, she stepped aside to let the others see. As Hunter moved past her, he saw a look of horror on her face, and his heart sank. A salt breeze pushed against him, as if trying to keep him from seeing.

Then, as he turned, he spotted Angerman on the beach, marching in the direction of the bunker. And walking in front of him was President, his hands in the air while Angerman held the gun to his back.

Chapter Eighteen

Mommy tried to make her lips move, but couldn't. No sound would come out of her. Had Angerman forgotten what they had told him about the vial of Fire-us? Or was he just too crazy to understand?

"*Angerman, no!*" Hunter shouted. But his voice was lost in the wind—or else Angerman was oblivious.

He and Teacher began running toward the beach. Mommy began running, too. They stumbled down the grassy hill, trampling daisies as they went.

Mommy pumped her arms, breathing hard. Did Angerman not get it? As soon as he shot President with Nana's gun the vial would break, releasing the Fire-us. And they would all be dead. All of them—except Teacher and the little kids, who hadn't gotten the pew-bertie.

Then Teacher would have to raise Teddy Bear, Doll, Baby, Action Figure, and the twins all by herself. And Mommy . . . she would never see her children again. No more bedtime stories and tucking them in. No more wiping grape jelly from their faces. No more watching them get bigger, stronger, smarter—and someday become real Grown-ups.

Realizing all this, Mommy was overcome with a grief so powerful that she opened her mouth and let out a loud, terrible howl, like an animal that had been shot. Hunter and Teacher froze and stared at her.

Angerman froze, too, and stared at Mommy. Across

the stretch of sandy beach, their eyes met. Mommy saw, even from that distance, that it was hopeless. Angerman was in another world. He barely seemed to recognize her. He didn't look like a boy anymore. He looked cold and hard and lifeless, like Bad Guy.

Just then, President turned and made a grab for the gun.

"Angerman, look out!" Mommy shouted.

Angerman whirled around. He wrenched the gun away from President and smacked him across the jaw with it. President reeled back and fell, kicking up a cloud of sand and pebbles and shells.

"The vial, where's the vial?" Hunter cried out.

Angerman took a step back and pointed the gun at President's head. The boy was shaking and crying.

"Angerman!" Teacher screamed. "Don't shoot!"

President staggered to his feet and said something to Angerman that Mommy couldn't hear. Angerman lowered the gun to his side. Just beyond them, a huge wave crashed against a big black rock. A flock of sandpipers rose in the air, frantically flapping their wings.

More words were exchanged. Angerman took a step toward President, put one hand on the man's shoulder, and spun him around. He jabbed the gun between President's shoulder blades, forcing him forward. They resumed their march toward the bunker.

Mommy saw President touch the pocket of his jacket before raising his arms in the air. "He still has the vial," she whispered to Hunter and Teacher.

Hunter nodded. "Come on—we've gotta stop Angerman!"

The three of them rushed toward the bunker. They

took a shortcut over a dune overgrown with sea grass and beach plums. As Mommy ran, she felt tears burning her eyes. She squeezed them shut, thinking about the little kids. Where were they now? Were they scared? Were they calling out for her?

This was all her fault. *Her fault.* She had let Angerman into their home, into their lives, back in Lazarus. And now he was going to cause the end of the world—*again.* The little kids were going to have to watch big kids and Grown-ups die—*again.*

Mommy, Hunter, and Teacher reached the bunker door at the same time as Angerman and President. Angerman was humming "Hail to the Chief." His eyes were swollen with tears and crazy looking.

President's gaze fell on Mommy. "Tell your friend to get his hands off me," he demanded. He had a bloody cut on his jaw where Angerman had smacked him with the gun. He ignored a fly that swooped around his head.

"Angerman, *please,*" Mommy said, panting. "This isn't—it wasn't what we—"

"Angerman, come with us," Teacher pleaded. She hugged The Book to her chest. *"Just do it!"*

But Angerman didn't even seem to notice that they were there. Still humming, still keeping the gun pointed at President's back, he kicked the bunker door open. An awful, musty smell wafted out from the dark cinder-block walls.

Angerman tapped President on the shoulder with the gun. "Welcome to your new home! I mean—where are my manners?—welcome to your new home, Mr. President, sir! Not exactly the White House, is it? But, hey, it'll be a very cozy place to spend eternity."

"You must be insane if you think you can get away with this," President hissed.

Angerman grinned from ear to ear. "I learned from the best! But don't worry, Prez! You're not going to spend eternity alone. 'Cuz I'm going in there with you. Yes sir, we're gonna hang out in this here bunker together . . . you, me, and that vial of killer Kool-Aid you got there in your pocket. We can spend eternity together—or a week, anyway—quotin' Bible verses and Dow Jones averages and maybe playing some Go Fish. You know Go Fish, Prez?"

Mommy gasped. Angerman wasn't going to shoot President. He was going to go into the bunker *with* him and release the Fire-us, killing them both. "Angerman," she whispered.

"This just in!" Angerman cried out, kicking the bunker door wider and forcing President into the opening. "Today on Pisgah Island—that lovely vacation spot known for its sandy white beaches, pretty girls, and lively bonfires—President J. Colin McDowell got his just desserts! And we're not talking ice-cream sundaes, folks! The Prez issued an official apology for murdering billions of people with Fire-us, the virus we all love to hate, for the sole purpose of—let's see what the press release says here—for the sole purpose of 'cleansing the world and making way for the Second Coming.' Gosh, can't wait to see what old Colin's got planned for the *Third* Coming! But there probably won't be time for a Third Coming, since the president's schedule is chock-full. For starters, he has made a recommendation to boost the ailing Georgia economy by offering himself as alligator bait. *What a guy!*"

"Give me the gun, Proverbs 6:27," President growled over his shoulder.

Angerman laughed. "Proverbs 6:27? Isn't that the name your Keeper slaves gave me back at the Crossroads?"

"Angerman, let's just go," Teacher whispered.

"No, no, this is good! You know what that is, Proverbs 6:27? *'Can a man take fire in his bosom, and his clothes not be burned?'*" Laughing, Angerman shoved President in through the open door. "You know what the answer to that is? No! A man *cannot* take fire into his bosom without his clothes getting burned. You're gonna burn, baby, burn! Happy Judgment Day, Mr. President! *Now get inside the bunker before I blow your brains to pieces!*"

"You can't kill him, Angerman, he's your father!"

President turned and stared at Mommy. Everyone was staring at her. Mommy realized that it was she who had spoken.

"Y-you're President's son," Mommy told Angerman in a small voice. "He's your father."

President leaned against the doorway of the bunker, as if to steady himself. All the color had drained from his face, and he seemed to be at a loss for words. "You're—"

"Hi, Dad!" Angerman said cheerfully. "Sorry if I don't offer to give you a hug."

"I thought I saw a resemblance, but I didn't dare hope . . . that is, I thought the three of you had . . ." President's voice trailed off.

"You thought the three of us had died, along with all the other people you murdered?" Angerman said. He flashed his old Anchorman smile. "This just in, Dad! As soon as Mom figured out what you were really about, what you were up to with your Great Flame Zero Population Economic Revitalization Plan, she took Sam and me and tried to run away. Highways jammed with cars, mass chaos and panic, mommies and daddies trying to escape with their kids, everyone burning up and dying—you get the picture. But let's cut to the chase: Mom and Sam got the Fire-us, too. I had to watch them burn up and die in an abandoned Winn-Dixie. Mom spent her last hours crawling through the aisles looking for food and water for me. Did you know that, Dad?"

"Mary—" President whispered.

"Do not say her name, do you understand? You have no right to speak her name," Angerman rasped. "Do you know what she said, at the end? She told me that everything was gonna be all right. She told me that Sam and she were going to the angels, and that they'd watch over me always and forever and make sure that nothing bad happened to me. Then she held Sam and me in her arms and sang that song . . . you remember, Dad, the one she used to sing to us when we were little . . . 'All the Pretty Horses.' She somehow managed to hold out until Sam . . . until Sam died. And then she . . . and then she . . ."

Angerman began crying again. Mommy began crying, too. Her heart was breaking for poor Angerman.

Sobbing, Angerman raised the gun in the air. President flinched. "W-what do you think you're doing?" he demanded.

"I knew all along. I knew it," Angerman said, his voice cracking. "Deep down, I knew. That's why I had to go to Washington. I had to find you and make you pay."

"You *knew* President was your dad?" Hunter blurted out. "Why didn't you tell us?"

"I don't know. I didn't always know it or believe it. It doesn't matter now." Angerman pointed the gun at President's head. "I changed my mind, Dad. I decided I don't want to play Go Fish with you, after all."

President pulled the vial of Fire-us out of his pocket. "Do you know what you're doing?" he said, his voice hardening.

"'*Fear God, and give glory to him; for the hour of his judgment is come. Yea, though I walk through the valley of the shadow of death, I will fear no evil.*'" Angerman cocked the gun. "Been real nice knowing you—"

"Don't do it, Angerman!" Teacher sobbed. "The Fire-us will kill you and Mommy and Hunter and—"

Teacher saw the shadowy movement on the other side of the bunker. At first she thought it was an animal, but then she saw that it was a soldier in a gray uniform. Teacher blinked through the haze of tears. It was Cory.

Before Teacher could say a word, Cory rounded the corner and rushed Angerman from behind. She grabbed him, then grabbed his gun.

"Hey!"

Startled, Angerman fumbled his grip. Cory wrenched the gun out of his hands.

Angerman whirled upon Cory with a look of pure fury. "What do you think you're doing?" he spat.

Cory met his gaze. She smiled, then raised the gun in the air and pulled the trigger. The sound was deafening.

President smiled, too. "Corinthians 1:19, you arrived just in time."

Teacher's heart sank. Cory had signaled the other Keepers. Once a Keeper, always a Keeper. But how could she do that to them? How could she do that to Puppy and Kitty?

From a distance, Teacher was aware of footsteps and shouting. The Keepers had heard the shot. Soon she, Mommy, Hunter, and Angerman would be surrounded.

"The rest of you are going to be very sorry for this," President said with a dramatic sigh.

The Book felt as if it were burning in Teacher's arms. She glanced down briefly, and saw that the pages had fallen open. Words leaped up at her, like fire:

Seal not the sayings of the prophecy of this book:
for the time is at hand.
Don't worry, be happy!

Teacher's head was heavy as stone as she looked up at Cory. Cory was smiling at her. Her eyes shiny with tears, she mouthed the words: *Good-bye.*

Wait a second, Teacher wanted to say. But before she had a chance, Cory flung herself at President, knocking him backward into the bunker. The vial of Fire-us flew out of his hand.

"*Wait a second!*" Teacher shouted.

Cory jumped into the bunker after President, grabbing the doorknob as she went. The last thing Teacher, Mommy, Hunter, or Angerman saw before the door slammed shut was the vial of Fire-us about to crash into the cinder-block wall.

"Cory!" Mommy screamed. "*Corrrrrrry!*"

Through the bunker door came the sound of a muffled shot. Teacher threw herself against the heavy door and pounded her fists on it. "No! Cory, I was going to—"

There was a second shot. And then silence.

Chapter Nineteen

There was no sound but the shushing of waves and the whisper of sand rushing over the dunes. Hunter remembered, deep inside his Before Time memory, that the earth was always spinning like a ball in space; and now he imagined the ball slowing down, slower and slower, and stopping. What would happen now? Would they fall off the earth? Was the world over? A sudden breeze drifted sand across his shoes, beginning to bury him. He knew he was crying, because his cheeks felt cold where the breeze cooled his tears.

Then Angerman let out a high-pitched wail. "What have I done?"

"He was going to kill Puppy and Kitty," Hunter said with difficulty. "They're his own kids, and he was going to kill them. So Cory—Cory—"

"People are coming," Teacher whispered, her voice thick with tears. She stood stiff and stunned, only moving her eyes toward the compound.

Mommy pressed herself against the door and hammered on it with her fists. "Cory! Cory, can you hear me!" she yelled. There was no sound at all from inside the bunker. "Cory, answer me!"

From the corner of his eyes, Hunter could see the distant shapes, a line of people running toward them. He stumbled forward to take Mommy's arm. She jerked it away from him, refusing to acknowledge him.

"She's dead. They're both dead," Hunter said. "And besides, even if they're not, we can't—we couldn't open—"

Mommy whirled around, her eyes wide and unseeing. "Are you crazy? If she's hurt, she'll need . . ." She trailed off, and Hunter saw her swallow hard.

"Fire-us," he said. "We can't let it out."

Mommy sank to the ground, covering her face with her hands, as the first two Keepers dashed toward them.

"What happened?" the taller of the two yelled. "We heard a shot! Where is Supreme Leader?"

Hunter wiped his hands across his wet cheeks, and tried to stand up straight and brave. "Fire-us has been released inside the bunker, and Supreme Leader is in there with it."

The two Keepers flailed their arms as they stopped short and stumbled against each other. The second one darted a wide-eyed look at the closed door. "He let it out?"

"It was his plan." Hunter lied.

But already the two men were edging backward, their faces rigid with fear. As one, they turned and began to flee, running headlong into the oncoming Keepers.

"Run! Our leader is dead, burned by the Great Flame!"

"The Flame is burning!"

There was immediate panic among the Keepers, and what had been a determined rush toward the bunker now became a desperate scramble to escape. Hunter, Teacher, Mommy, and Angerman watched without speaking. The Grown-ups who had followed President McDowell so confidently were now scattering across the island like a flock of sparrows harried by a hawk. Hunter was quite certain that very soon, they would all be gone, running for their lives, getting as far away from the Great Flame as they possibly could. And with no leader to guide them, to think for them, to make their decisions, they would be on their own and helpless. Hunter turned away in disgust.

Teacher was on the ground beside Mommy, cradling her as they both cried for Cory. Hunter imagined President, on the other side of the door, either dead of a gunshot or dying of the virus, and his heart cried out *We're free!*

And he began to cry in earnest because they were more alone now than they had ever been in all these five years.

Dazed, Angerman tipped his head back, watching the clouds hurry out to sea. Each one was tinged apricot-gold on its western edge, and strong shafts of light from the setting sun speared seaward. Like a holy picture, Angerman thought, like the pictures in the Sunday school books, where the light beams were supposed to be a symbol of God. Sometimes, when he was little, he had confused *Our Father* with his father, and wondered if the charismatic man he called Dad was really God.

And obviously, he hadn't been the only one to get confused about it. Angerman heard a man's voice like an echo, and a howl of rage and pain boiled up his throat. He wanted to smash his own head against something, the way he had smashed Bad Guy so often, wanted to crush out all the memories that rose up like disgusting phantoms in his sleep, gibbering and mocking him. *Your father, your own father!* He had been trying so hard for all these years not to remember this, and he thought maybe he *had* gone crazy trying to forget. His father, his own father had killed the world, the one who was supposed to protect him and keep him safe. It was unbearable. Maybe he should have known this sooner, should have done something to stop him way back before the virus. His father had killed the world, and now Cory was dead, and maybe that was his own fault, too.

In the midst of his howling, Angerman felt arms around him. Mommy, and Teacher, and Hunter all held him in a close huddle, standing shoulder to shoulder. And then Mommy did an amazing thing. She said his real name.

Chapter Twenty

"David, David, David . . ."

Mommy murmured his name over and over again. She felt Hunter's arms and Teacher's arms and Angerman's—David's—arms around her. She pressed her face into someone's shoulder and breathed in the salty smells of sweat and ocean and tears. This, *this* was real. David's name was real. Everything else was gone from this world—names, TV shows, ballet recitals, First Mommies and Daddies, sisters, brothers, and now, Cory, too—but at least they had this, they were alive. Their little family could go on.

And then Mommy remembered about the rest of them, and jerked away from the warmth of the huddle. "The children! We gotta find the children!"

"Teddy!" Teacher gasped, almost dropping The Book.

David swiped a hand across his eyes. "Come on, let's go."

The four of them scrambled up the hill toward the main compound, Mommy in the lead. The trees and grass looked blue in the twilight. A single star twinkled in the sky. Mommy's muscles ached, and her stomach hurt from the blood, but she didn't want to slow down. The thought of her children alone and terrified—or worse yet, in danger—made her feel crazy with panic. *Don't delay!*

They soon reached the top of the hill. In the distance, Mommy could just barely make out dozens of lights, bobbing up and down. The Keepers were making a mass exodus for the bridge.

Then Mommy heard them—heard Doll's high-pitched cries and Puppy's yips and barks. "Listen!" she cried out.

Teacher, David, and Hunter stopped at her side. "What?" Hunter said breathlessly.

"Don't you hear them? Doll and Puppy. The others must be with them."

David shook her head. "I don't hear anything."

"Listen!" Mommy craned her neck.

Leaves rustled in the breeze. Crickets whirred. A twig snapped as a small animal scurried through the woods. Then a single word pierced the air and lingered there: *"Mommy!"*

The four of them took off running again. The voice—Baby's—came from the direction of the meeting hall.

When they got there, they saw that the double doors were closed and bolted. Nearby, Doll's one-eyed dolly was lying in the grass, next to a broken spear. Stifling a cry, Mommy scooped the dolly up in her arms and rushed to the door. She threw the bolt open and jiggled the knob.

It wouldn't give. "*Kids!* Are you in there?" she shouted.

"Mommy!" Baby screamed.

"Teddy! Are you guys all right?" Teacher yelled over Mommy's shoulder.

"Teacher!" came Teddy Bear's muffled cry. Fists began banging on the door from inside.

"I can't—I can't get the door to open," Mommy cried to the others.

"Here." Hunter brushed past her and tugged on the knob. "Action, are you in there? Unlock the door!" he shouted.

"We tried! We can't!" Teddy Bear replied.

David eyed a high-up window. "I'm going in through there," he said.

Hunter nodded. "Yeah, all right, good. That's a good plan." He ran over to the window and dropped to his knees. "Here, Ang—I mean, *David*. Leg up."

David gave Hunter a look of surprise. "Okay."

Hunter cupped his hands over his mouth and yelled, "We're coming in through the window, so stand back!"

The banging stopped. "'kay! Over and out!" came Action Figure's voice.

Mommy pressed her ear against the door. She heard the mad scramble of footsteps, and Action Figure barking, *"Move it, move it, move it!"*

David put his right foot on Hunter's hands, then his left. He hoisted himself up onto the ledge and smashed the window in with his elbow. Pieces of glass crashed onto the floor inside.

Careful of the jagged edges still stuck to the frame, David crawled through the hole, then disappeared over the edge. Mommy heard a squeal of happiness—Baby's—then a jumble of voices shouting: *"Angerman, Angerman!"* A few seconds later there was a small *click*, and the door swung open. Teddy Bear burst out with a wail, then Action Figure, then Doll and Baby.

The girls threw themselves at Mommy's legs. Mommy bent down and buried her face in their hair. "It's okay, everything's okay now," she murmured, her voice cracking.

Mommy glanced up through the tangle of blond curls and saw David standing in the doorway, holding Puppy and Kitty. Seeing the twins' tearstained faces, Mommy's heart tightened in her chest. How were she and David and Hunter and Teacher going to break it to them that Cory was dead? Did they even understand what death was? They had watched their First Mommy, Ingrid, lie down in bed one day and not wake up. Now, Cory wasn't going to wake up, either. How would they take this news?

Mommy was about to say something to David when she saw his lips curl up into a smile.

Mommy was startled. What on earth did he have to smile about? "What is it, David?"

"David, who's David?" Doll demanded. "And where is my dolly?"

David nodded down at the twins, who were rubbing their eyes with dirty fists. "Hunter said they were . . . *his*. Right?"

Mommy nodded slowly. "Right."

David's smile widened, and a single tear rolled down his cheek. "This just in! Puppy and Kitty are my little brother and sister."

Moonlight poured through the window and made David's bedroom silvery white. Teacher shifted her weight slightly so she could see better in the darkness. She was careful not to wake Teddy Bear, who was curled up on her lap. The girls, Action Figure, Puppy, and Kitty were also asleep, sprawled out on the two twin beds.

Mommy, Hunter, and David were sitting cross-legged on the windowsill, talking in quiet voices.

It was David's old room—the one he and his older brother, Sam, had shared during their vacations on Pisgah Island. David had remembered the wallpaper with the small blue seashells, the white rocking chair, the old wooden desk. He had even found a place on the side of the desk where he had carved his name in tiny, crooked letters: *DAVID McDOWELL.*

Teacher sighed in wonder at this—a real name from the Before Time! She picked up her pen and wrote across an ad for allergy medicine:

> David McDowell.
>
> He came to us in Lazarus and led us on our Journey. Now President is dead, and so is Cory. Where will we go now?
>
> Nana said I'm Sorry about a million times and asked us to come back to the Woods with her, to live with the grandmas. But we decided we can't do that. If she hadn't given the little kids to the Keepers maybe Cory would be alive right now. We need to find a different place to live. A safe place with no Grown-ups. But where?
>
> We need Answers.

Teacher turned the page. There was a magazine picture of a girl in a uniform, kicking a soccer ball. Across it, Teacher scribbled:

Cory Cory Cory.

She bent her head and began crying, trying not to wake the children. Teddy Bear stirred in her lap, grunted, then was still again. Someone squeezed her shoulder and whispered her name. She glanced up and saw Mommy smiling down at her. David and Hunter were standing on either side of her.

Mommy wrapped her arms around Teacher from behind. "Hey. *Hey.*"

"What are we gonna do?" Teacher said, sniffling. "Where're we gonna go?"

"Should we go back to Lazarus?" Mommy said. But before anyone had a chance to reply, she said, "No, uh-uh, that's a bad idea."

David ran his hand across the top of the desk. "Um, well, we could go to my house," he suggested in a shy voice.

Teacher sucked in a deep breath and turned the pages of The Book until she got to page 34. She pointed to a brochure with a big white fancy house on it, and the words: *OUR NATION'S CAPITAL.*

"You mean *this* place?" she said. "The White House in Washington, D.C.?"

David shook his head. "No, my *real* house. Where we lived before my father became president. It's in Washington, the state."

Everyone was silent. "That's far away, isn't it?" Hunter said finally.

"Yeah," David agreed. "Everything's far away, though. We could try. Do you want to try?"

There was a pause, with everyone thinking their own thoughts. Teacher sat up and began flipping through the pages of The Book. There had to be a map in here somewhere that would tell them how to get to this other Washington.

Outside, a cloud passed across the moon. Teddy Bear murmured "*balloon,*" then nestled his body into Teacher's. He was so heavy, he was getting so big. Then the cloud passed, and the room was bright with moonlight again, and Teacher saw that she was on the last page of The Book.

It said:

Blessed is she that keepeth the sayings
of the prophecy of this book.

WE'RE STILL HERE.

Fridays at seven!

KIDS GET IN FREE!

"Teacher, what is it?" Mommy whispered. "What does The Book say?"

"I think it means we're gonna be okay," Teacher replied, feeling the relief wash over her. "I think that's really what it means. I think we should go."

Good evening! And now the news.

This morning, Nana, an M.D. who may I say also happens to make a mean goat cheese salad, freed several dozen Keeper women—sorry, folks, I meant *girls*—and their babies from a prison on Pisgah Island. The girls had been kept there by a man known as Supreme Leader. Some of you may remember him by his pseudonym, President J. Colin McDowell. The girls had been part of a selective-breeding program engineered by McDowell, who thought that the world might be a better place with a New Savior who had his eyes, his bone structure, and his awesome sense of humor. The babies—ranging in age from five weeks to twenty-two months—were all his spawn. But we're not going to be hearing from McDowell again, folks, and the girls and their babies are on their way to the Woods with Dr. Nana to start productive new lives. The best of luck to you all!

In other news, a group of kids were seen leaving Pisgah Island today. They've spent several swell days vacationing there, but in the words of one of the guys, "It was time to be moving on." Before leaving, the kids were seen placing a wooden marker near the beach. Carved on it were the words: CORY YOU WILL BE WITH US FOREVER. Puppy and Kitty left a bunch of daisies there, and the girl known as Doll left her dolly—"so Cory wouldn't be lonely." Very nice touch!

The kids—ten of them in all—were last seen heading west. The weather should be good for traveling: low 80s, 0 humidity, a slight breeze from the south. Bon voyage, kids! Have a safe trip!

Oh . . . and by the way, this will be my last newscast for a while. I'm going on a long-overdue vacation. With my family.

3-24-24